MW00775015

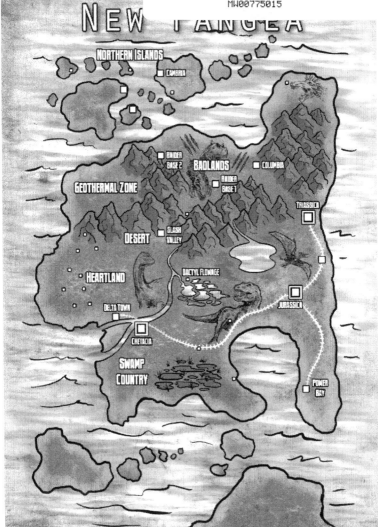

COME FOR THE DINOSAURS, STAY FOR THE HUMANS.

As dynamic and fascinating as the prehistoric beasts of this novel are, they are far outstripped by their *Homo sapiens* counterparts. With *Carnivore Keepers*, Kevin M. Folliard creates a fascinating world where people and dinosaurs cohabitate on the continent of New Pangea; a world where survival is the first order of business, and business is booming.

One part *Mad Max*, one part *Jurassic Park*, and one part *The Great Escape*, this novel is not just another post-apocalyptic man vs. dinosaur romp. While there is hair-raising excitement, fast-paced action, and blood-chilling violence, there is a surprising amount of intrigue, personal drama, and political strife. And, as alluded to before, the real stars of *Carnivore Keepers* are Folliard's fully realized characters, the heroes and the villains.

If you're in the market for "something completely different" and you have a penchant for sci-fi, action, adventure, and good old-fashioned, edge-of-your-seat storytelling, I highly recommend Kevin M. Folliard's *Carnivore Keepers*, and I hope you enjoy your stay in New Pangea.

~ Jason J. McCuiston,
author of *Project Notebook* and The Last Star Warden series

CARNIVORE KEEPERS

BY
KEVIN M. FOLLIARD

From
Dark Owl Publishing, LLC

Arizona

Cover image and map by James T. Molloy
https://jamestmolloy.storenvy.com
On Instagram @jamestmolloy

Cover design by Dark Owl Publishing

Visit us on our website at www.darkowlpublishing.com

ALSO FROM DARK OWL PUBLISHING

Novels

The Keeper of Tales
An epic fantasy adventure by Jonathon Mast

Just About Anyone
High fantasy comedy from the twisted mind of Carl R. Jennings

The Black Garden
The beginning of the dark mysteries within the town of Ste. Odile
by John S. McFarland

The Malakiad
A hilarious mythological misadventure by Gustavo Bondoni

The Wicked Twisted Road
A gritty, grindhouse sci-fi thriller by D.S. Hamilton

The Mother of Centuries
The continued haunting tale of Ste. Odile's mysteries
by John S. McFarland
Coming October 2022

Anthologies

A Celebration of Storytelling
The anthological festival of tales
Something Wicked This Way Rides
Where genre fiction meets the Wild West

Collections

The Dark Walk Forward
A harrowing collection of frightful stories from John S. McFarland

The Last Star Warden:
Tales of Adventure and Mystery from Frontier Space, Volume I
The first in the series of the Star Warden's adventures
from Jason J. McCuiston

The Last Star Warden Volume II:
The Un Quan Saga
More chronicles of the Last Star Warden by Jason J. McCuiston

No Lesser Angels, No Greater Devils
Beautiful and haunting stories collected from Laura J. Campbell

Tension of A Coming Storm
Horror and terror within a dark mass of short stories
by Adrian Ludens
Coming September 2022

Young Readers

Grayson North, Frost-Keeper of the Windy City
A totally cool urban fantasy adventure by Kevin M. Folliard

Dragons of the Ashfall
Book One of the War of Leaves and Scales
Steampunk fantasy adventure from Jonathon Mast
Book Two is coming soon!

Shivers, Scares, and Goosebumps
Short tales to chill you to your bones
written and illustrated by Vonnie Winslow Crist
Coming September 2022

Annette: A Big, Hairy Mom
A touching story of a boy and his motherly friend, a Sasquatch
written and illustrated by John S. McFarland
Coming October 2022

Available on Vella

The Last Star Warden: The Phantom World
Eight episodes of nail-biting sci-fi action from Jason J. McCuiston

Buy the books for Kindle and in paperback
www.darkowlpublishing/the-bookstore

More titles are planned for 2023 and beyond!

PROLOGUE

Caleb crouched in cliffside brush as the sun sank behind the red ridges of the badlands. There wasn't much cover, but the boy was small for thirteen. And he had been practicing quiet, controlled breaths. A dragonfly landed on his nose and crawled up his face. Caleb remained still.

Below, his bait limped and crowed with pain. Caleb had snatched the furry *Rhamphorhynchus* off the roof of the compound storage garages where it had landed to catch insects. *The hunter becomes the prey,* he had thought as he broke one of the pterosaur's leathery wings. Its squeals had sent pangs of guilt through Caleb. He had never deliberately injured a creature before. But New Pangea was a cruel continent. And the mining settlement of Columbia had been established on the outskirts of its cruelest territory.

Now the meter-long pterosaur circled the maroon cove on the edge of the badlands, screeching and dragging the diamond vale of its tail. The injured pterosaur's cries would draw his true quarry. As the sky darkened, inevitably *Deinonychus*—*slashers*—came hunting. Caleb wanted more than anything to kill one, and he had planned this trap for weeks, chosen this perfect spot along the rocky wall.

The *Rhamphorhynchus* flexed its jaws and crawled on crooked wings. The prey would be too small to attract the attention of a pack. But Caleb hoped it would be too tempting for a stray *Deinonychus* to pass up. He was right.

A long shape, feathered in bright red, stalked on two legs around the rocky bend. She had a toothy snout, moon-yellow eyes, and three-fingered hands. Each foot sported a curved sickle claw. Her stiff tail balanced behind her. The animal stood tall as a grown man and stretched three meters lengthwise from snout to final tail feather. The *Deinonychus* snarled and cocked her head at the injured pterosaur.

The *Rhamphorhynchus* attempted flight with its useless wing and chittered with fear. Guilt twisted Caleb's stomach as the *Deinonychus* strode forward, head bobbing. She snatched up the helpless creature with clawed fingers and chomped over her writhing head. With a bony crunch, the *Rhamphorhynchus* slackened.

Caleb clutched his father's hunting knife. The handle was tyrannosaur bone, the blade iron from Columbia's mines.

Days before his parents' deaths, Caleb's father had been cleaning the knife when Caleb asked how the raiders managed to tame *Deinonychus*. His father told him of a man he'd met once who laid traps for dromaeosaurs of all kinds in the south. The man would lurk in trees, lure the predators with something small but tempting, drop down, and wrestle the animals into submission. The man had pinned *Velociraptors* and *Troodons* and claimed that, after sparing their lives and giving them food, the predators respected him.

Three meters below, the *Deinonychus* chomped a few more times and started to swallow the pterosaur whole. *Now or never,* Caleb thought. He clutched his father's knife and dropped.

Caleb tackled the *Deinonychus*'s back. She grunted with surprise and collapsed to one side. Caleb wrapped his arms around her neck, legs around her middle. The animal shrieked and kicked. She craned her neck back, snapped and snarled. A dusty cloud swelled.

The *Deinonychus* was much bigger than a raptor or *Troodon*, and Caleb was smaller than the man his father had known. He wasn't strong enough to hold on long enough to subdue this beast or earn her respect. But he didn't want a monster's respect.

Caleb tightened his grip. The *Deinonychus* wrenched her body. Her free arm snatched back and tore Caleb's shirt.

The boy's heart pounded. It took every ounce of his strength to keep the dinosaur from righting herself. *I can't do this,* he realized. *The second I position the knife, she'll break free.*

The predator's right arm continued to slash back. She snatched the collar of his jacket and pulled. Her neck reached back. She was tugging him toward her snapping jaws.

Caleb tensed his whole body. The *Deinonychus* chomped air. Her rotten breath washed over him. Her teeth were stained with pterosaur blood.

He felt the animal pause for a breath. In that moment, he unhooked his right arm from her torso and stabbed the *Deinonychus*'s throat.

The predator choked and rasped. Blood gushed over Caleb's fingers. The animal twitched, and then lay still.

Caleb remained in strange embrace with his prey until he managed to catch his breath. Then he got to his knees and wrenched his father's knife free. More blood spilled over his pants. He stood on shaky legs and examined his red, trembling palms. He hadn't thought about the blood. He had nothing to clean himself with.

It didn't matter. There was no one at home who would be concerned to see him return tonight, stained with dinosaur blood. The people of Columbia had bigger problems than the dangerous games of one orphan.

The boy spit on the dead predator. True, it was not the one that had killed his parents, but nevertheless he smiled with the satisfaction that he *could* kill one. He would keep killing slashers. He was going to get better at it. And soon, he would hunt the humans who tamed them.

1

"We're not building walls for you." Ambassador Niles Stanton straightened his back and folded his hands.

The Triumvirate of Columbia glared at him from across the oak table. Behind them, a landscape painting of the fledgling quarry town depicted how the colony had been meant to evolve over the past five years.

The painting's stylish apartment towers and quaint cobblestone town square was a far cry from the bamboo food centers and shanty towns that still made up Columbia. Gray-backed *Pteranodons* circled the air over the mountains in the mural's upper right corner. The left side depicted the edge of the badlands where a pack of fiery-feathered *Deinonychus*—what locals liked to call slashers, due to their deadly sickle-shaped toe claws—foraged for prey.

If only the dinosaurs had been the biggest threat to Columbia.

The three leaders exchanged stony expressions. Edmund Patel furrowed his brow. Allianna Martin's gaunt fingers curled together, her eyes narrowed, and the creases on her elderly face deepened. But Joe Nash merely slumped and shook his head.

"Why not?" Allianna's icy accusation cut the silence. "On what grounds is Triassica breaking their promise?"

Stanton maintained his steely resolve, but his gray suit was starting to itch. Sweat beaded beneath his dirty blond crew cut. "Triassica is not breaking any agreements. We sponsored Columbia on the pretense of resource sharing, expansion, and promotion of stability across New Pangea. In five years' time, Columbia's mining operations have failed to yield the flow of minerals and building materials that we invested in."

"We will never meet those demands," Patel said. "Not without walls. Invest in a reliable barrier. Help us keep the raiders at bay, and in time, we will all prosper."

Stanton slid a red folder across the table. "This is our current offer of temporary support. We will provide additional security forces which will remain with the compound for a transitional period of one year, leaving Columbia with weapons. Columbia will continue to receive food rations for the next six months."

Patel opened the folder and paged through the agreement. "These rations are pitiful. Columbia's population has not dwindled this much."

"They're cutting us off, Edmund," Allianna said. "Is our plight so inconvenient, Ambassador? Does it make Triassica's councilors quake with guilt while they sip champagne at the Ludlow Opera House—"

Stanton held up his hand. "Ms. Martin, there is no need for hostility."

She raised her voice, "—lording over the worker ants! Is it so difficult to empathize—"

"Allianna, please!" Joe finally spoke. "Ambassador Stanton is our voice to Triassica. He deserves respect. And he has not made this decision... not alone, at least."

For a moment, Stanton met Joe's gaze, but he couldn't hold his poker face and bear the heartbreak in those brown eyes. Stanton glanced away to clean his reading glasses on his pocket square.

"If Ambassador Stanton represents this deal, he has lost my respect." Patel tossed the red folder back to the center of the table. "They are leaving us to die. We suffer near weekly disturbances from the raiders. They pilfer when we're lucky. They murder when we're not. And sooner or later they will come in great numbers. We were promised the support of Triassica."

"Under contingency," Stanton said. "And you have not met those requirements."

"We can't, Niles!" Joe shouted. "Try to remember for one second that we are talking about people. It's easy to forget that when you have a high rise overlooking the ocean, with a steady flow of food and supplies."

"Joe," Stanton said, "this is not about... me, okay?"

"We have had to *beg* Triassica for everything, the same compound that sponsored us, that petitioned for ten percent of its citizens to found this colony." Joe raised his voice. "You personally encouraged me to serve on this Triumvirate. So, yes. It is about you."

Stanton took a deep breath. His palms sweat.

"Columbia is failing," Joe's voice broke. "Hundreds of lives are at stake."

"What do you have to say to that, Ambassador?" Allianna's

crystal blue eyes fixed on his. "That it isn't your problem? That you don't have the authority? That Columbia's shortcomings are a sign of *our* failings as leaders? Would you like to try to run this colony without walls for five years? Do you think the losses—the death toll—would be lower under *your* supervision?"

"Ms. Martin, I am deeply, personally, sorry for all that Columbia has suffered. But that," he pointed to the red folder, "is currently your best offer. Accept it, and then we will see what else can be done."

"I am eighty-five years old, Ambassador Stanton." A smile crept across the woman's face. "In New Pangea, that's beyond ancient. I owe my privileged longevity to compound politics, of course. But I've seen and known enough to learn that sooner or later, living a life of genuine service to others, I would be chewed up and spit out."

Allianna leaned forward and spit on the red folder. "I am grateful at least that for me, it was later."

"Ms. Martin—"

"What about the children out there? Living in tents. Hungry. Covered in dust from the badlands. Raiders—horned devils— haunting their nightmares."

Stanton took a shaky breath. "I cannot help you any further at this time."

"Fine." Allianna leaned back. "But if you leave this room, without renegotiating, you will not be welcome back."

Stanton stood. "I will relay your refusal to the Council of Triassica." The ambassador quickly gathered his materials and travel pack. "Good day." He hurried through the double doors of the meeting room, down the long, white hallway of the colony's administrative center. His footsteps echoed.

The doors burst open behind him. "Niles!" Joe hurried after him. "Niles, stop!"

"What more is there to say, Joe?"

Joe grabbed his shoulder and pulled him around. "I'm telling you this not because you deserve the warning, but because you are still my friend: You cannot leave. You'll die."

Stanton studied Joe's resolve. "What do you mean?"

"I mean, you have to promise to do everything you can to recommit Triassica to the walls."

"Or what? That crone will have me shot? She knows I have no sway on the Council. I'm a middleman. You know that better than anyone."

"This is what I've always told you," Joe whispered in anger. "So stubborn, and yet so complacent."

"I didn't come here to dig up our personal failings."

"Grow a backbone!" Joe shouted. "And try." Stony silence filled the hall. "Please, not for me," Joe said. "For your *own* sake. Triassica has to understand how futile it is operating out here. All our manpower goes to defending ourselves, and they think we can mine for them? It's insane. It was their idea to come here."

Niles placed his hand on Joe's shoulder. "Columbia was a good idea. But it's hard to predict these kinds of obstacles."

Joe shook his head. "They *knew* about the raiders."

"They knew of gangs in the badlands. Cultists who worship the carnivores," Niles said. "Nobody knew they were this organized or ruthless."

Joe stifled tears.

"Joe, really, I *am* sorry. We should never have invested in this colony, and it's too late now."

At last Joe's tears broke free. Niles reached for him, but Joe held up his hands to keep him away.

"Fold the colony, Joe. Start transitioning citizens back to Triassica and the other major compounds. There will be a waiting list, but I can get you to the top. Patel and the old woman, too. The Council isn't as heartless as she thinks."

"You think I would abandon these people?" Joe shook his head. "Maybe you're not the man I loved anymore, Niles. But I am begging you not to walk out that door."

Stanton turned toward the glass doors to the sunlit rotunda. "There's nothing to renegotiate, Joe. What is she going to do? Have me shot on the way back to my vehicle? Is she so spiteful?"

"It's worse than that."

A long, deep noise echoed outside, sorrowful and ghostly. It didn't sound like any dinosaur he had ever heard.

Joe whispered, "It's the raiders' war horn."

A chill ran down Stanton's back. "They're here?"

"I didn't know until just before our meeting, but Allianna's intelligence predicted an attack. It's why she pushed up negotiations. She wanted you to see what they do. To live through it. To completely understand the urgency of our situation."

The deathly horn resounded. Then a low roar echoed outside the walls.

The double doors to the meeting room burst open, but Patel and the old woman did not appear. Instead, two guards armed with pulse rifles flanked the doors. "We're on lockdown, Mr. Nash. We need you behind as many doors as possible."

Joe smiled sadly and turned toward the meeting room.

Outside, people screamed. The sharp cracks of pulse rifles echoed.

Stanton attempted to follow Joe, but the guards armed their weapons with twin electric hums. "Ambassador Stanton, you are not permitted on the premises. By majority rule of the Triumvirate, you are to leave the colony or be shot on sight."

"What?" Stanton shouted. "Joe, talk to them. I'm not going out there in the middle of a raid!"

Joe faced him one last time before retreating behind the double doors. "What can I say, Niles? I'm overruled. You know how that goes, don't you?" Joe slipped away. The guards filed in after him, and the door locks reverberated down the hallway.

Outside, more shouting and pulse rifle fire sounded. The raiders' war horn blared again. Stanton cautiously approached the glass doors. The admin who had greeted him that morning had abandoned her post, gone into the colony's defensive drill. Stanton struggled to remember the drill. The safest bunkers were in the center of town and, of course, under the administrative center, where guards would certainly shoot him on the order of that hag Martin.

The colony had no walls, but they did have crude defenses: fencing, barbed wire, sandbag blockades, and rifle towers that faced the badlands. Stanton's transport crew was waiting on the southwestern edge of Columbia.

His crew knew the negotiations would be quick, and they were ready to leave at a moment's notice. But could he make it there fast enough to avoid the raiders and their pets?

Stanton hurried out the glass doors, into the rotunda. A deafening roar rattled the windows. A huge shadow swooped past the skylight windows. Stanton glanced up in time to spot the dark shadow of a passing *Pteranodon*. The huge, winged pterosaurs could be dangerous, but as far as anyone knew, they weren't part of the raiders' menagerie. They did have a habit of following the raiders, though, to pick at the carnage they left in their path.

More rifle fire cracked outside. Fear pumped through Stanton's chest. *Get a grip,* he told himself. *Before compound life, you dealt with constant danger. This isn't any different. You haven't gone that soft.*

He took a deep breath and pushed through the doors.

Outside, carnivores snarled louder. Rows of tents and utility shacks blocked the western side of the colony. Large trucks and jeep engines hummed in the distance.

With bigger, louder dinosaurs, and large enough trucks to cart them, the raiders were surely out in full force. This wasn't a small pack. It was an army.

2

More cracks echoed from Columbia's rifle towers, followed by an explosion that shook the air. A series of crumbling snaps reverberated. Then black smoke plumed behind the row of tents, right where a guard tower had stood.

Stanton bolted southward, around the central compound. Groups of panicked citizens hurried eastward between the alleyways of the mineral sorting tents. Suddenly, stacks of lumber exploded from the right, blocking Stanton's path. A huge, charcoal-colored animal with red bumps on its back lurched forward. Stanton ducked into a nearby tent and hid behind a stack of ore crates.

The animal snorted and kicked at piles of lumber. Stanton cautiously peeked between the crates. The dinosaur stood over three meters tall, over eight meters long. He had a stubby snout with rows of sharp teeth, and twin V-shaped horns. Armored plating ran down his back onto a thick muscular tail. *Carnotaurus.*

From what intel Columbia had gathered, the raiders had a system of bonding with predators like *Carnotaurus*. Stanton studied the predator's twitching front claws and huge bloodshot eyes. His pupils appeared dilated.

They drugged him, Stanton realized. *Hyped him up and unleashed him on the town.* It was consistent with the raid reports he had reviewed from the safety of his office in Triassica. The raiders brought their animals to the colony, riled them up, unleashed them, and plundered food and resources during the chaos.

The *Carnotaurus* snarled in the direction of the panicked crowd. It kicked up dust and sprinted down the alley. Stanton climbed on top of the ore crates. He retrieved a pocketknife from his travel pack and slit an opening in the tent above, then he cautiously tore his way up to look around.

He could make out the tips of *Carnotaurus* horns stalking the southern end of the administrative center. On the western front, raiders covered in red war paint and bone tattoos shouted and cheered. Lines of quad bikes and motorcycles faced Columbia. Six huge cargo trucks faced the rifle towers. A few were already open. Stanton spotted two more black and red *Carnotaurus* tearing through sandbag blockades and barbed wire.

More trucks opened up, and more Carnotaurs stomped onto the grass, wild-eyed, tiny forearms twitching. Electric blue bolts of energy fired from the rifle towers, but the drugged-up predators didn't seem to feel the sting against their armored hides. The raiders blew their war horns again. The line of leather-vested soldiers cheered from their quad bikes.

Stanton turned his attention southward. His entourage would be waiting beyond the southern supply garages. He could still make it while most of the raiders' forces were focused on the rifle towers and blockades.

But once the towers fell, nowhere in town would be safe.

Stanton climbed back down. He ran and leapt over fallen lumber. To the left, he glimpsed the massive horned beast gnawing at a light fixture. The war horns blared again. Screams echoed from the guard towers. The electric hum of the raiders' quad bikes grew louder. Rifle fire split the air.

Three enormous *Pteranodons* swooped overhead. Stanton hastened to the rendezvous point. His heart pumped as he quickened his pace. He only had to round the utility garages. If they left immediately, if they were lucky, the raiders would never even notice them.

As he approached the gray brick walls of the garages, a terrible crunching sounded. Glass shattered. Someone's screams were cut short. It came from the south.

Stanton stopped, breathless. Then he spotted a chrome-colored shape flipping in the air. It crashed in front of him. Cracked solar panels lined the severed hood of his own vehicle. A large animal snarled from the other side of the garages. More crashing, crushing sounds echoed. Devilish black horns poked from the other side of the garage.

There was no ride home.

3

Stanton's stomach sank. He was stuck in Columbia.

His mind raced to figure out the next option. He knew Columbian officials kept the keys to their own long-distance vehicles in the administrative center. He couldn't commandeer one without going all the way back and dealing with the Triumvirate again.

The safety bunkers were also guarded by Allianna Martin's soldiers, all instructed to shoot him.

Wood and metal crunched and clattered. Stanton whipped around to find one of the raiders' trucks backing up, tearing between two supply tents. Crates split and spilled iron ore. The back of the truck was lined with thick metal bars. The truck halted, and the gates opened.

Stanton raced to the access ladder on the back of a nearby supply garage. Loud, angry chirps echoed as he climbed. He tore the sleeves of his suit as he pulled himself over the edge of the garage's roof and rolled onto gravel.

He took a moment for his heart to slow down. Then he peeked over the ledge and watched as a pack of fiery red *Deinonychuses* poured from the truck, eyes wild, toothy snouts snapping at air.

Their three-fingered hands flexed with excitement.

The *Deinonychuses* chittered amongst themselves in a strange dinosaur huddle, and then the pack dispersed. Stanton rolled onto his back as two scampered in his direction. To the south, the *Carnotaurus* growled and crunched something near where Stanton's support team had been. To the north, feathered pack hunters snorted and sniffed.

He spotted a flat, gray rectangle on the next roof over, a trapdoor into another garage. The supply garage doors weren't exactly *Carnotaurus*-proof, but at least down there he would be out of sight.

Stanton hopped the narrow gap between the garages. He crept low toward the hatch, when suddenly a rush of air blasted him in the face. Something thumped onto the trapdoor, blotting out the sun. A huge, gray-crested *Pteranodon* sat in the center of the roof, wings spread. Her toothless beak poked toward him.

"I'm not dead yet, stupid!" Stanton kicked at her face.

The *Pteranodon* squealed and snapped.

"Get out of here!"

The *Pteranodon* crawled forward on folded wings. She squealed again.

"Shut up!"

Predators on either side of the supply garage chirped and snorted. The *Pteranodon* was getting their attention.

Stanton scooped a fistful of gravel and hurled it at the pterosaur's face. The winged creature ducked and snapped. Stanton stumbled backwards, nearly stepping into the gap between the garages.

Curious chittering sounded below. Suddenly a *Deinonychus* leapt onto the rooftop. The predator tilted wild, yellow eyes at Stanton, then at the *Pteranodon*.

The *Pteranodon* squawked and flapped enormous wings, washing hot air over the roof. The *Deinonychus* snarled as the pterosaur took off, and Stanton scrambled for the trapdoor. He pulled the gray hatch open, just as the *Deinonychus*'s claws slashed toward his hand. He pulled away. A red streak cut across the back of his hand.

The *Deinonychus*'s toothy smile widened. The animal's partner leapt up to join him.

Stanton held his hands out to protect his face. The *Carnotaurus* growled from behind. High above, the shadowy *Pteranodon* circled, waiting for what the *Deinonychus* would leave behind.

This was it.

The trapdoor burst open with a clang, and in an instant, a hooked object impaled the *Deinonychus*'s eye. Blood squirted. As quickly as it had appeared, the weapon yanked free. A short figure stood, silhouetted by the blazing sun, clutching a pickax. "Come on!" a young voice shouted.

Stanton followed his savior through the trapdoor. He pulled it shut, just as the second *Deinonychus* lurched forward. Stanton tumbled over a stack of sandbags, onto the concrete floor of the supply garage. Above, the *Deinonychus* screeched and clawed at the hatch.

"That should hold," the young voice whispered. "Stay quiet. There's a bull-head out there." A sandy-haired boy, no older than thirteen, motioned to the black and red armored hide outside a cobweb-crusted window.

They waited in silence until the large predator stomped away.

"Thank you," Stanton whispered. "If you hadn't arrived—"

"Why aren't you with the others in the safety drill?" The boy whispered. "This is not the best place to be."

"Long story," Stanton said. "How about you? Shouldn't you be with your parents?"

The boy glared. "My parents are dead."

"Oh. I... I'm sorry. You must have a guardian who's looking for you."

The boy studied Stanton's clothes. "You're from Triassica."

Stanton nodded.

"You're here to negotiate." A faint smile lifted the boy's dust-crusted face. "Once we have walls, those raiders are done for."

Stanton's heart sank. "Is that what the Triumvirate promised?"

"Yeah. How fast are they going up? Raiders pick us over once a month. Sometimes more. Why didn't you come with more people?"

Stanton's voice shook. "I... was really only here to discuss terms. My transport crew, they were..." He gestured toward where the *Carnotaurus* had stood.

The boy nodded with grim understanding.

"What's your name?" Stanton asked.

"Caleb West."

"Caleb. I am so sorry for what you've been through. My name is Ambassador... uh, Niles Stanton. And I really want to do everything I can to help Columbia. The raiders are—"

"Shh!" Caleb held a finger over his chapped lips.

Stanton held his breath. Distant shouting was muffled by the garage door. The *Carnotaurus* was now on the other side, growling and snorting. The *Deinonychus* on the roof scraped the metal hatch.

"I see Number 7 on the roof!" An icy voice drew nearer. "Tell round-up. Must be a dead pterosaur up there. 8 ran off, far as I can tell."

The *Carnotaurus* roared. The garage door rattled. Outside the window, Stanton could once again make out the large predator's torso some distance away. A tiny, clawed arm tensed into attack position.

"Knock it out, Bessie! I see that raspberry jam on your lips." The raider laughed. A loud hum sounded. "You ate already. Now back up, Bessie! Back away, that's right!"

The man gave a series of brisk whistles. The enormous predator growled and lurched forward.

Sparks sounded. The *Carnotaurus* snorted and twisted away, showing her stubby snout.

"That's it, now! Back 'round front!"

Combat boots appeared in the crack at the bottom of the garage door.

A radio crackled. "You get Bessie moving, Whistler?"

"She's fine. Wandered down here to guzzle up some blokes waiting outside the compound. Trashed their car, too. Shame about that. Might be worth salvaging, but I don't think we have the room. Solar panels are shot anyhow, thanks to Bess. Quite a mess."

Stanton's stomach turned. *If only they hadn't waited for me,* he thought. *If they had left the second they heard the raiders' war horn…*

Vibrations rattled the garage door as the *Carnotaurus* stopped nearby.

"Those *Deinonychuses* got up on the roof, though," Whistler said. "Low flying *Pteranodon* started a fight or something. Looks like he's picking at something. What you got up there, 7?"

The *Deinonychus* chirped.

Stanton and Caleb exchanged nervous glances. The dinosaur knew there were people in the garage. What would the raider do if he knew?

"Round-up is on the way," the radio crackled. "Get 7 down from there. When they get obsessed, they don't listen."

"Looks like he's digging," Whistler said.

The *Deinonychus* snorted and scraped the hatch.

"He's trying to get inside. What do they keep in these south garages?"

Caleb slowly hoisted his pickax and aimed it toward the soles of the man's boots.

The radio crackled. "Nothing good last time, just old tools, sandbags. The ore and food are already being loaded."

"Still." Whistler's boots shifted. "Maybe they moved something around. Could be more food here. Medicines and such. Maybe even something Necra could use to cook up something nasty."

The radio crackled and the raider on the other end chuckled.

Caleb clutched the handle with both hands. The head of the ax trembled.

Stanton spotted a wrench on the wall and reached for it.

Calloused hands, with tattooed fingers curled under the garage door and slowly pulled it up.

As soon as the door passed the raider's scuffed black boots and khaki pants, Caleb swung the pickax into the man's thigh. Blood spurted. Whistler shouted. Caleb wrenched his weapon away and backed up.

Stanton pulled the boy behind him, clutched his wrench.

The man swore and screamed. His blood-soaked legs quivered. "Number 7!" he shouted. "I have a treat! Number 7! Treat!" He gave a long, low whistle.

Clawed *Deinonychus* feet stomped in the dirt next to the raider. "Get 'em, 7! Eat 'em up!" The raider pounded the garage door. "Food inside!"

The *Deinonychus* crouched. His toothy jaws flexed as he crawled under the opening.

Stanton took a cautious step forward and swiped at the dinosaur's snout. The *Deinonychus* snapped in retaliation. Stanton pulled back, but the predator managed to snatch the wrench from his grip.

The *Deinonychus* pulled through and leapt at Stanton.

Caleb jammed his pickax into the animal's eye. The *Deinonychus* shrieked and fell onto his side. Sickle-shaped foot claws thrashed the air; his feathery tail banged the metal door. Caleb pulled away, but the ax remained lodged in the animal's eye-socket. Blood speckled the boy's arms.

The bald raider, with a tattooed collar of teeth around his neck, yanked the door the rest of the way up. His one pant leg was soaked red. He wore a dinosaur-hide jacket over a bare chest, tattooed with curved slash marks. "7 was my favorite!"

Whistler lurched toward the boy. "You hurt one of our babies, eh?" He grabbed Caleb by the wrists. "We'll hurt one of yours!"

Caleb shouted. He struggled for a knife strapped to his ankle.

Stanton dove for the wrench and whacked Whistler's skull. The raider stumbled but didn't fall. An electric hum sounded, and before Stanton could react, the raider jammed a shock prod right in his gut.

Electricity coursed through him. Stanton convulsed, collapsed, and spasmed on the ground.

The boy shouted. The room spun.

Sharp pain cut across Stanton's back. The injured *Deinonychus* was kicking him.

"Your old man's gonna pay, kid!" Whistler growled. "That was enough juice to herd a *Carnotaurus*."

Caleb screamed something, but Stanton couldn't make it out. His vision was fading. Turning white.

More dark shapes appeared, silhouetted against the sun, more raiders, screaming and shouting. Stanton tried his hardest to focus. To get up. For a moment, his vision cleared.

Behind the approaching raiders, he saw the wreckage of his transport vehicle, flipped completely upside-down. A pool of blood leaked from the driver's side.

The approaching raiders wore barbed metal claws on their wrists.

"Gut him!" The raider whistled, long and low. "Tear out his insides! Let's make his boy watch!"

4

Caleb's eye swelled with pain as he drifted in and out of consciousness. The sun burned his face. All around him, the raiders' convoy rumbled. He struggled to move, but his limbs were bound tight to a cargo net on the back of one of their jeeps.

His good eye blurred into focus. High above, shadowy *Pteranodons* soared, following the line of trucks.

Caleb struggled to piece together what had happened. *Why did they take me?* he wondered. *Why am I not dead?*

He remembered rescuing the Triassica ambassador and the fight in the supply garage. The raider had his claws ready. He was going to kill the ambassador. Caleb dove for his injured leg. More raiders showed up.

They pinned him up, took his father's hunting knife, and hit him so hard he saw stars. He remembered hearing them talking over their radio about Triassica, but then the next thing he knew, he was tied to the back of the quad bike.

"My father's knife!" he shouted. "I want my father's knife!"

"Shut it, brat!" a gruff voice shouted over the hum of the engines.

"I need my father…" he winced with pain. "Took my knife…"

"Shut up about your father!"

To his right, he spotted the armored shape of a *Carnotaurus* hide between the bars of a cargo truck. The blazing red rocks of the badlands were all around them, the roads were rough in patches, but they seemed to be following a trail of some kind.

They rounded a bend in the rock and Caleb spotted a clearing that stretched between the mountains. In the distance, two enormous rocky plateaus pillared, side-by-side.

"The horns!" the driver shouted. "Home with spoils!" The raiders' war horns blared, and Caleb took a closer look at the twin mountains. They did indeed look like *Carnotaurus* horns, a dark gray color in contrast with the reddish hues of the surrounding terrain.

He spotted vehicles between the mountains, and a hole, a rectangular cave at the base of the left horn. Along the sides of the horns were scaffolding and ropes.

The raiders started to chant:

Under the horns!

Under the horns!

Yo ho! Yo ho!

Under the horns!

Life is good! Between the horns!

"Give it back!" Caleb screamed over the raiders' noise. "My father's kni—"

Something squeezed his neck from behind. "I said shut up about your dad! Shut up altogether!"

Caleb gagged as rough hands shoved him. For a moment his body lurched off the edge of the cargo net, but his bonds held him in place.

The *Pteranodons* soared lower. Their enormous wings blotted the sun. Caleb's head swirled with vertigo. And he blacked out once more.

5

Stanton felt cold stone. His head throbbed. The cuts on his hand and back stung. He opened his eyes.

A five-by-five-meter concrete room appeared through a haze of dizziness.

Filthy liquid dripped and pooled in one corner. He attempted to stand, but rusty chains crossed his chest, pinning him against some kind of stone support pillar. A windowless, metal door faced him. Above, a fluorescent bulb buzzed.

Stanton's gray suit was torn, stained with blood and dust. His tongue felt heavy. His mouth dry. The scene at Columbia came flooding back to him.

That ice queen Allianna Martin.

Joe leaving him to die.

The boy in the garage.

Stanton had expected the Columbia ultimatum to be the most unpleasant task of his career. But until now, he hadn't truly allowed himself to be in their shoes. To appreciate what the situation had devolved into.

A lock unlatched. The iron hinges of the door creaked open. A tall, muscular man with buzzed gray hair—a raider—appeared from a dark hallway. He wore combat boots, khaki pants, and a leather vest. His belt holstered a tranquilizer gun and shock prod on either side. A bandolier with tranq darts crossed his bare chest.

The raider's arms were inked with dinosaur bones, like the others. But over his eyes, twin *Carnotaurus* horns were tattooed in a V shape. Pointed teeth formed rows above and below his human mouth, forming the cruel, permanent smile of a carnivore.

Stanton studied the man under the fluorescent light. Beyond the plastered dinosaur grin, his true expression was difficult to read. But he looked old for a raider—perhaps late forties.

The man said nothing for a long while. He merely locked eyes with Stanton.

Finally, Stanton spoke. "What do you want with me?" His voice came out hoarse.

The raider's human lips curved into a smile that matched the tattooed jaws. "I haven't decided yet. You don't seem frightened."

Stanton shrugged. "I'm tired."

"No, that's not it." The man stared for a while longer. "Something's missing. Men in your situation tend to feel desperation."

"I'm thirsty. Injured," Stanton said. "I guess I'm in shock. I don't know."

"I don't think you are." He rubbed his chin. "I'll figure it out, Ambassador Stanton." He produced Stanton's ID badge from inside his vest and tossed it on the concrete floor. "Triassica sent you to check on their little project?"

Stanton stared.

"We like the food you send." The raider circled the pole and reappeared on Stanton's left. "And we like the mines you built. But we'd like our mountain back."

"It was never your mountain. You people never ventured this far east before."

"Well, there was no mine then. Now there is."

"Because *we* built it. You're thieves." Stanton braced himself for retaliation.

Instead, the raider shrugged. "We're opportunists. Most people consider *Deinonychus* and *Carnotaurus* to be monsters. My people saw companions."

"You drug your *companions* and unleash them on innocent people. You're not just thieves. You're murderers."

"What you call a murderer, I call an opportunist. You should respect that, ambassador. It's because I have vision that you are currently in this cell, instead of in the slurry we feed our pets."

Stanton's stomach turned. He inhaled deep and tried to regain his composure. The room was starting to spin.

"You sit chained in a cell and have the nerve to call your captors thieves and murderers. Is this truly how ambassadors from the compounds negotiate?"

Don't apologize, Stanton thought. *Show no additional weakness. He wants something. Find your leverage.*

Stanton glared at the raider. "I am afraid I did not catch your name."

The tattooed jaws leaned down. "I have no name. Only a title."

"Then I did not catch your *title*."

"I am the Alpha. I speak and make decisions for my pack."

"I respect that," Stanton said. "We take your people very seriously where I come from. We know you're strong, smart, organized."

"Please. You call us savages. You insult us."

"It would be an insult to grovel, to bore you with pleasantries," Stanton said. "When I call you thieves or murderers or savages, it's because I sense that you embrace those terms. You wear the bones of vicious animals on your skin with pride."

The Alpha's smile widened and stretched his tattooed teeth. He stood tall and folded his arms. "That is an impressive insight, Ambassador Stanton."

"I understand the position I'm in, and furthermore, I suspect you're a man who will appreciate bluntness." Stanton's cottony tongue scraped the roof of his mouth.

The Alpha produced a small canteen from his inside pocket and unscrewed the top. He started to hold it toward Stanton, but then he pulled back and took a long drink for himself. He screwed the cap back on and put the canteen away.

Ignore it, he told himself. *Thirst is not a part of this. You have to impress him right away. Earn his respect.* He cleared his throat. "I'd like to cut through all the minds games if we can. Why exactly did you spare me from the carnivore slurry?"

The Alpha unclipped his shock prod from his belt and fondled it. "Your little project next to the mountain is folding, isn't it? Personally, I've lost count of all our raids over the years, but there have been plenty. If Triassica hasn't fortified after all that, it means they don't consider Columbia worth the resources."

Stanton said nothing.

"We're patient. We've been waiting for you to leave, so we can set up our own special shop there once you're gone. The ore is great for building pens. See right now, we have to look for places, like this facility you're in now, nestled into the natural landscape."

"A cave system with gates and stone enclosures." Stanton glanced around the concrete room and noticed irregularities in the ceiling. The floor was sloping as well, where the puddle formed. "We assumed you kept your animals someplace like this."

"Metal has so many uses. The point is we're looking to expand."

"You're going to take the mountain once we abandon Columbia, and then you think you're coming south," Stanton said.

The Alpha's eyes widened. "I don't just think it."

"I don't want to lie or play to your ego, so I'll tell it straight: Triassica is formidable. Your dinosaurs and trucks," Stanton gave a hoarse laugh, "and *tattoos* are not going to get you anywhere close to the city. You don't have the numbers. You don't have the muscle. And I've seen your animals; they're fierce, but Triassica is a fortress."

"We intend to place someone inside that fortress."

Stanton studied the Alpha's face, which had once again gone blank. *He's not talking about himself. Does he have a loved one? A wife, child, sibling who needs advanced medical attention from a compound?* "I'm afraid I don't have the kind of authority that you think I do."

"We want *you* inside that fortress, doing favors for us."

"What kind of... This is moot. You don't understand Triassica.

Once I'm back there, what makes you think I'd deliver even if I agreed to your terms?"

"Because you're going back alone."

Stanton locked eyes with the Alpha. The carnivore horns arched over his eyes. *What does he mean? Is he taunting me because they killed my transport crew? Who does he think I'd be going back with? Joe? Does he know about Joe somehow?*

The Alpha snapped his fingers. The iron door creaked open again, and a second raider pulled the boy from Columbia in from the darkness. Caleb's arms were bound behind his back. His right eye was swollen purple. His face twisted into a stoic scowl. He was sniffling, desperately fighting tears.

"*You* go back." The Alpha smiled. "Your *son* stays here. If you fulfill our agreed upon favors, then we will return your son unharmed. Betray us, then—what's the boy's name? He's barely said a word."

Stanton took a deep breath and steeled himself. "Caleb. My son's name is Caleb."

"If you betray us, his name will be Slurry. Do you understand the terms of this negotiation now, Ambassador Stanton?"

He whispered, "I do."

"So, what is your answer?"

Tears streaked Caleb's dusty cheeks.

"I need time."

The Alpha recoiled with confusion. "Time?"

"To think."

"You need time to *think*? About your strapping boy's life?" He glanced between the sniffling boy and Stanton. Then he laughed long and hard.

"I need assurance of good faith on your part," Stanton said. "How do I know you won't kill him regardless of whether or not I help you? Let me talk this over with him."

"Gambling with your son's life." The Alpha bared his human teeth and leaned in close again. "You might be a savage too, Ambassador. No wonder you think you understand us."

The Alpha nodded at the other raider and jerked his head. The raider shoved Caleb into one of the filthy puddles. "Slurry—I'm sorry, Caleb, was it? He can stay for now. I will return *very* soon, and when I do, I expect full cooperation."

The other raider disappeared into the darkness. The Alpha started to follow.

"Wait!" Stanton called. "What are the demands? What are your favors?"

The Alpha gave a wry smile. "Who says I've thought of them yet?"

"We need water," Stanton said quickly. "And food. I can't make a decision if I'm dehydrated."

The Alpha gestured to Caleb, slumped in filthy liquid. "I was kind enough to provide you with a cell that came with water. I'm sure your son can help you get some. You can make a game out of it." He turned and slammed the iron door behind him. The lock clicked.

Caleb started to stand, and then collapsed back in the puddle. He leaned against the wall and cried.

"You told them I was your father?" Stanton whispered. "Why?"

Caleb shuddered. "I thought... I'm so stupid…" He broke down again.

"No, you're not stupid, okay. But we have to think fast."

Caleb cried harder.

"Caleb, come on! Are you the same kid who saved me with a pickax? Please, I know you're brave—braver than me—so pull yourself together and help me figure this out."

Caleb's breathing steadied, he sat up straight. "I'm sorry…"

"It's all right. What happened after I got knocked out in the garage?"

"I tried to get away, and they grabbed me. A raider hit me in the face. I was pretty out of it most of the way here. I woke up in a cell like this." He sniffled. "They told me I was going to see my father... I told them my father was dead." He choked back another sob.

Stanton's heart sank. "And they told you he was alive."

Caleb nodded. "And I believed them." He broke down again.

"They never found your dad's body? After the attack that killed him? You thought maybe he had been here all along."

Caleb sniffled, nodded.

"I'm sorry." Stanton's guts tightened. "Caleb, listen, we're in a horrible situation, but it's lucky that you played along up to this point. I don't know what these people will do if they realize we're not related. You might only be alive because someone noticed my badge and assumed you were my son because we were together."

Caleb sighed. "I really thought they meant my real dad…"

"I'm sorry about that. But going forward we need to be on the same page about everything, okay? If they suspect anything, they'll cross examine us, and they'll figure it out. They'll kill us if they think we have nothing to offer them."

Caleb nodded.

"Were you born in Triassica? Did your parents migrate to Columbia from Triassica?"

Caleb nodded.

"Do you remember the city? Your parents told you about what life was like there?"

"I was seven when we moved. I remember."

"Good, because as far as our story goes, you're my only son. We live in Triassica and travel to Columbia regularly. Your mother died in childbirth, and you never knew her. These are the kinds of basic facts we have to keep straight between us, but as a general rule, Caleb, I want you to go mute. Say almost nothing unless they threaten to hurt you. Let me do all the talking for us. The less you say, the less of a chance for us to contradict one another."

Caleb nodded. His shoulders slumped. He looked like he was about to pass out.

"Caleb?"

The boy raised his glassy eyes.

"Get out of that puddle, okay? Come here."

Caleb took a shaky breath, stood, and made his way to the center of the room. He sat next to Stanton.

"I want you to listen to me: I don't know what's going to happen. But I promise you, I am going to do everything that I can to get us out of here. Can I count on you to help me?"

Caleb stared blankly at the iron door.

"Caleb? Are you listening?"

"You asked me why I was out there," the boy's voice came in a far-off, dreamy tone. "Why I didn't go with the crowd when the drill started."

"Why didn't you?"

Caleb stared trance-like at the door. "I wanted to kill one of the things that killed my parents."

"You want revenge."

The boy nodded. "I got so good at it. Picking off those slashers. I would sneak into the badlands and wait for them. Get the drop on them. Get them right in the eye."

Stanton recalled how Caleb had felled two *Deinonychuses* with stunning accuracy.

"Mr. Stanton, I don't care if you get me out of here alive or not. I just want to kill one of them. One of the humans, I mean. I want to kill the man with the *Carnotaurus* face."

"Look at me, Caleb."

The boy locked eyes with him.

"Everything that I do, is going to be to get us out of here, safely. I don't want you antagonizing any of the raiders or being difficult. Follow my lead. Go with the program. Listen to them. Cooperate."

"I don't want to cooperate!" he shouted.

"Quiet!" Stanton snapped. Then he softened. "Cooperate *for now*. Until I figure out a better plan, okay?"

Caleb shook his head. "There's no getting out of here alive. Don't you know that?"

"I don't accept that, and neither should you. So here is my revised promise: I will do everything I can to get us out of here safely, and *if* in that process I determine that it's possible to also get you your revenge, then I'll help you do that too. Is that a deal?"

Caleb hesitated, then nodded.

"Good. Because we—"

Laughter echoed behind the iron door. An animal snorted. The unmistakable hum of a shock prod buzzed, followed by a high-pitched spark. More laughter erupted, getting louder, closer.

Caleb and Stanton watched as the door unlocked and creaked open. The Alpha entered first, followed by a two-meter tall *Deinonychus* wearing a wire mesh muzzle. Two raiders, a stoic man with a blazing red beard and a wiry woman with a black mohawk, entered behind the predator.

The Alpha smiled. "Hello, Ambassador Stanton, Slurry Stanton."

"That couldn't have been more than ten minutes," Stanton said, irritation creeping into his tone.

"I said I'd be back soon." The Alpha patted the *Deinonychus*'s back. "This here is number 24. She was from the same egg clutch as number 7. You might remember 7; your boy shoved a pickax right into his brain. 7 had to be put out of his misery. He's in the slurry now, but 24 might want revenge for what happened to her brother."

The *Deinonychus* scraped her claws on the concrete. Crimson feathers bristled on her neck.

The color drained from Caleb's face.

"So anyway, I was wondering if you boys had agreed to my terms."

The *Deinonychus* bared serrated teeth at the corners of her snout. Her clawed fingers twitched. The woman with the mohawk stroked the dinosaur's feathery back.

"I'll agree, given certain provisions," Stanton said.

"We have no interest in your provisions, Ambassador," the Alpha said. "You can tell them to 24 here if you want."

"I only ask that you listen," Stanton said. "Because how this works out affects both of us." Stanton caught himself, glanced at Caleb. "*All* of us."

The Alpha stared. The dinosaur's sickle claws scratched the concrete.

His silence is your opportunity to speak, Stanton realized. *You might not get another one.* "It's important for me to understand the nature of your favors, even if you reserve the right to change or adjust them later. Obviously, you want me on the inside to weaken Triassica's defenses somehow or otherwise help you access our resources. I get it."

The Alpha tilted his head. "Is there a *but* coming, Ambassador? Because 24 doesn't care for—"

"*However*," Stanton raised his voice. "You have us in a no-win situation. If I do something to bring Triassica to ruin, and let's assume you follow up on your promise and return my son safely, what is he returning to?"

"Let's assume the worst," the Alpha said. "New Pangea is a big continent. Change your names and go someplace else. Some nice settlements far south, I hear. Plenty of adventure in the Northern Isles."

Stanton continued, "And what condition will I find Caleb in upon his return? Physically. Psychologically. Look at how you've been treating us."

"I gave you a cell with light and water." The Alpha shrugged. "You could have been slurry. You could have been dropped in the arena for sport. For an outsider in our culture, this is downright hospitable."

"Well, if you expect me to abandon my *son* to this place, then I'm going to need you to go well beyond hospitable. At the very least, I need assurance that you will treat him with the same privilege and respect that you afford the other members of your *pack*. For starters, how about some food and clean water, if not for me, then at least for him."

"You're a bold man, but not a very good father, Ambassador Stanton." The Alpha reached down and snatched Caleb by the arm.

The boy shouted and struggled, but within moments, the Alpha had him pinned against his chest. He turned to the two handlers. "Ajax, Necra, I think 24 needs to stretch her jaws."

The woman with the mohawk whispered in the animal's ear and stroked her neck. The man started unstrapping the muzzle.

"Stop!" Stanton said. "Just *listen* for one minute, please!"

The Alpha grabbed a fistful of Caleb's hair and pulled his head back. He held the boy's tanned neck toward the *Deinonychus*.

Caleb grimaced and squeezed his eyes shut.

"You don't make good spies by strong-arming and terrifying

them," Stanton said. "You assure them. You incentivize them. The kind of service you're asking of me requires some degree of mutual respect."

The Alpha nodded at the bearded man. "Ajax."

Ajax slipped the muzzle off the animal. 24 stretched her jaws, revealing rows of serrated teeth and a long pink tongue. The woman Necra scratched the dinosaur's chin, cooed to her.

"I'm agreeing to work for you, in the interest of my son's life," Stanton said. "But I... I need you to let me stay here—with him— for a few weeks. So he can adjust. So I can see what life is like here, how he'll be treated, what I'm leaving him to."

Necra purred and whispered in a strange raspy language. 24 licked her lips.

"If you convince me that Caleb will be okay here," Stanton said, "then I'm much more likely to serve your demands. Doesn't that make sense to you?"

The Alpha's blank expression finally broke. His eyes narrowed into angry daggers, made all the more terrifying by his horned brow. "You are playing with fire, Ambassador!" he shouted. "You don't make demands of us!" He yanked Caleb's exposed neck closer to the animal.

The *Deinonychus* salivated. Necra soothed: "Not yet, 24, not yet."

"I agreed!" Stanton shouted. "Please! Let him go!"

The Alpha snarled, "You're going to learn the hard way that you are not in charge in this place, Ambassador!"

Caleb trembled in the Alpha's iron grip.

"I understand. *You* are in charge," Stanton said. "Absolutely.

These are *not* demands that I'm making, okay? They are... suggestions. I think it will be good for *all* of us, if you and I have a strong, working relationship. That takes at least a small measure of time to build. I'm asking for that time, here, on your terms, under your roof."

Silence hung in air. The *Deinonychus* chittered with excitement, binocular eyes fixed on Caleb's throat.

"Necra," The Alpha said. "Go get 24 a treat."

"Come on, girl." The woman yanked the animal away from Caleb. The *Deinonychus* hissed and struggled as Ajax wrapped his hulking arms around her long neck. Together, Necra and Ajax managed to reattach and secure the muzzle. They led 24 back into the dark hallway. Her growls echoed.

The Alpha still held Caleb against his chest. "Take a look at your boy, Ambassador. It might be the last time you see him." He pulled Caleb into the dark.

"Wait!" Stanton shouted.

Caleb screamed as the iron door clanged shut.

6

The huge raider named Ajax dragged Caleb, kicking and screaming, back to his holding cell. Caleb waited there in darkness. He closed his eyes, counted the minutes, and dreamed of gutting them all: Ajax, the woman Necra, the raiders from the supply garage, and their leader with the *Carnotaurus* face.

He struggled to free his wrists, but the bonds were iron tight.

Ajax soon returned with another female raider, a muscular dark-skinned woman with no hair and *Deinonychus* feathers tattooed over her shoulders. She carried a metal case. Ajax had a wooden chair in each hand that he set in the middle of the holding cell. "Sit down, kid," he said.

Caleb glared.

Ajax tensed. "I said sit!" He pointed at the chair.

"Why?" Caleb asked.

Ajax loomed over him. Caleb took in the toothy markings that circled his bald head, the long bone-shaped tattoos over his muscular arms. He snatched Caleb by the collar and lifted him effortlessly into the air. "Listen... Caleb. You are going to learn quickly to do as I say, because I guarantee you, going forward, what I tell you to do will always be for the best."

He lowered Caleb to his feet. "Now sit in that chair and stay still. Because the alternative is that I tie you to that chair. It will not be comfortable, and quite frankly, I don't enjoy tying kids to chairs."

Caleb opened his mouth, but then he remembered his promise to Ambassador Stanton. *Cooperate. Say as little as possible.*

He sat across from the woman. She opened her case and retrieved a handheld metal object. She flicked it on, and it buzzed.

Hair clippers.

"Sit still," the female raider instructed.

Caleb gritted his teeth as she shoved the clippers across his scalp. Shaggy blond clumps fell into his lap. She ran the clippers across his entire head, around his ears and the back of his neck. Golden hair piled at the base of his chair.

Once the woman was done shaving Caleb's head, Ajax rubbed his reddish beard with approval and said, "Give him a sickle through the eye. Just one."

The woman shook her head then pulled a long, sharp object out of her case.

Caleb's heart pounded. "What do you mean a sickle through the eye?" He pictured his pickax going through the *Deinonychus*'s eye in the supply garage.

Was this torture? Retribution?

"He hasn't earned this," the woman said.

"Take it up with the Alpha," Ajax said. "One through the eye. It'll look good."

"It disgusts me," the woman said.

"Just do it."

"Do what?" Caleb attempted to stand.

Ajax pushed him back down. "Sit still!" The raider's sturdy grip pinned Caleb's shoulders in place.

Caleb wriggled his head and neck. "No!"

"This will hurt," Ajax said.

"Let me go!" Caleb cried.

Ajax wrapped one massive arm around Caleb's torso and secured his head between his hands. The woman leaned forward with a long needle in one hand.

"Do it!" Ajax shouted. "One through the eye!"

***

Stanton awoke to cool liquid pooling in his throat. He coughed, gagged, and cleared his windpipe. He tried to lurch forward, but found himself still chained to the pole.

"Drink!" a harsh voice shouted. Strong fingers pressed his shoulders. The metallic rim of a canteen was forced into his mouth.

Stanton eagerly slurped and sucked cool liquid. He had no idea how long he'd been without water or when he had most recently lost consciousness. The last thing he remembered was the Alpha's tattooed face grinning, his human face scowling, as he dragged Caleb into the shadows.

He inhaled through his nose as he sucked up every drop of water he could get.

"That's enough." Necra, the female raider with the mohawk, pulled the canteen away. "I have jerky. Eat." She held out a strip of dried meat.

Stanton wondered what kind of jerky it was only after he'd chewed and swallowed. It tasted like salted rubber, but his stomach grumbled for more. "Why don't you unchain me?" his voice came out a scratchy whisper. "I can feed myself. It's not like I could get past you people, let alone escape from this cell."

"You're a prisoner." Necra fed him another morsel of jerky. "Prisoners wear chains."

As he chewed, Stanton examined the *Pteranodon* beak tattoo that protruded from the base of her mohawk down her forehead. The black ink appeared to lead down the back of her neck and connect to the claws of pterosaur wings that covered her shoulder blades.

He swallowed. "What am I eating? Retired *Carnotaurus*? First you enslave them, then you unleash them on people, then you eat them?"

"It's food." She crinkled her pierced nose in disgust. "Be grateful." She fed him another bite.

As Stanton swallowed, his stomach felt uneasy, but not because of the food. *You're so busy keeping a stiff upper lip that you forgot to ask about Caleb,* he realized. *That should have been the first thing you did when you regained consciousness. It's what his real father would have done.*

Necra's cold eyes studied him as she tore more strips of jerky. If she thought it odd that he hadn't asked about his son—who could very well be dead or injured—she wasn't showing any sign of suspicion.

"Thank you… for the food," Stanton said. "Can I…" *Know who you're dealing with,* he thought. *This woman is part of the pack. She's not in charge.* "Please deliver a message to the Alpha for me. I would like to speak to him about my son's safety, and about how I can best... be of service to him... to all of you."

"The Alpha will see you when he wants to see you." Necra held out another strip of dried meat.

Stanton opened his mouth.

The woman withdrew the food and ate it herself. "That's all you get." She headed through the exit, then paused. "It was *Deinonychus* meat, the one your son slew back at your settlement. That may be the last food you ever eat."

The iron door clanged.

7

Stanton wasn't sure how many hours he spent listening to the hum of the fluorescent light and the drip-drops falling into the puddle.

He occupied his mind running through every possible scenario. What would he do or say if Caleb still lived? If the boy was dead? How would the Alpha react to various questions, attitudes, or ideas? Had his initial instinct to come on strong, bold, to earn the raiders' respect been wrong after all?

Moreover, what were the Alpha's favors likely to be, and how could he leverage them?

The nagging doubt of Caleb's safety haunted him, but too much time had passed. *Maybe they hurt him*, he thought, *but why would they kill him? I wouldn't still be alive if Caleb was dead. They're playing games. Just games…*

Stanton dozed on and off. Before long, his incredible thirst returned. His stomach cramped with renewed hunger. The cuts on his back stung. The slashes on his hand had scabbed into hard black lines.

At last, the lock clicked. The iron door swung open, and the Alpha stood, a lone figure, half in shadow.

"Caleb," Stanton wheezed. "Where's my son?"

The Alpha strolled forward, a double carnivore grin stretching his cheeks. "We will talk about Caleb."

He didn't call him Slurry, Stanton noted. *Is that a good sign?*

"First, I need you to answer a few questions."

"Can I have more water?" His tongue scraped the sandpaper roof of his mouth. "I can barely speak."

The Alpha sighed. "You drive a hard bargain, Ambassador." He produced his canteen, squatted, and grabbed Stanton's chin. His nails dug into Stanton's skin as he tilted his head back and poured water down his throat.

Stanton tried to block out the pain, to focus only on gulping as much water as possible without gagging. He managed to get a few gulps down, then once again, liquid clogged his windpipe and he hacked it back up.

The Alpha stood and took a swig for himself. He waited for Stanton to finish coughing. "Is that better?"

Stanton nodded.

"Where is the central control area for Triassica's power grid?" the Alpha asked.

Stanton feigned concentration for a moment as he calculated how compromising this information could potentially be. "Close to the northern interior perimeter. Off the top of my head, I don't have map coordinates. Furthermore, I don't have access. It's not in my job description to—"

"Just answer the questions I ask, Ambassador Stanton." The Alpha raised his eyebrows, his hand rested on his shock prod. "How many exterior perimeters are there?"

Tell the truth, Stanton thought, *but focus on details that would discourage an invasion.* "One main wall, plus a northern checkpoint built into the city's natural defenses."

"I know about the mountain gate," the Alpha said. "So just one wall after that circles the whole city?"

"Two walls including the interior perimeter. Like I said, it's a fortress."

"Is there an armory?"

"Several."

The Alpha paused. "Which you do not have access to, I take it?"

"I know people, but I would need a very good reason to get in."

"I'll bet someone like you is already thinking up three or four reasons."

"I've already thought about them, while sitting here, chained in your cell. Your lovely cell, with light and water."

The Alpha laughed. "You are a good negotiator, Ambassador. I'm beginning to like you. What kinds of weapons?"

"The most advanced pulse rifles in New Pangea. You could punch a hole through a T. rex with them. We're the gatekeepers of the south, you know."

"So I've heard. The men on your walls, they carry these rex-punchers?"

"Some of them do, yes. They're mostly a deterrent. Every now and then, security has to fire a few weaker charges to repel big dinosaurs away from our infrastructure, though by now it's rare that any of the local wildlife considers Triassica their territory."

"But if my crew and I showed up at that north gate, you'd blow a hole through all our pets."

"And your trucks and your jeeps. And probably all of you."

"And if I showed up at your gate with my crew, and a knife to *your* throat, are you important enough that anyone would care to hear me out?"

"No," Stanton said. "They'd just take the shot."

"Ruthless." The Alpha circled the stone pillar. "Heartless."

Suddenly, the chains went slack. Stanton collapsed on the concrete as his binding unwound. His back ached. He groaned with stiffness.

The Alpha reappeared in front of him. "Stand." He tossed the canteen at Stanton's chest. "Have another drink. I want to show you something."

Stanton's hands trembled as he unscrewed the canteen top and chugged what remained. Then he shakily got to his feet. His head swam with dizziness.

"Follow me." The Alpha was already disappearing down the shadowy hallway. Stanton stumbled after him.

"Are we going to see Caleb?"

"Don't ask questions," came the Alpha's hardened voice from the darkness. A flickering blue light silhouetted his muscular frame as he turned a corner.

Stanton struggled to make his weary legs hold him upright, to move one foot in front of the other. He pressed against the stone-cold wall for support. As he rounded the corner, more lights shone from a wider opening. A musty odor permeated the cool air.

The Alpha waited at the end of a stone hallway, bathed in blue light.

Stanton cautiously approached and emerged at the edge of a metal catwalk. Below them, a cavernous opening stretched deep and wide. Torches and electric lights were fixed to the stone. Metal staircases and scaffolding lined the walls.

Machinery echoed from the other side of a stone pillar in the center of the cavern. Somewhere, a chorus of *Deinonychuses* chittered. A *Carnotaurus* snorted. Traces of animal dung lingered in the air.

Supply crates were arranged below. Many of them Stanton recognized from Columbia, with Triassica's *Dimetrodon* emblem stenciled on the side.

At the far end of the cavern, a crew of five raiders were guiding a horned, bull-faced *Carnotaurus* through a gated opening, the tips of their shock prods glowed at the ready, but the animal was cooperating.

Stanton scoured the cavern for signs of an exit, a glimpse of daylight or the night sky, but all he spotted were mysterious openings in the rock, some gated, others that led into dim or black tunnels. He wondered how deep underground they were, but he knew better than to ask more questions. Except of course for the one a father would not be able to suppress. "Please," he said. "Take me to Caleb. Prove to me that he's all right."

The Alpha glared. "You're not impressed by all of this, I know. Triassica is more advanced, but we're proud of our operation here."

"Others saw a hole in the ground, and you saw a base of operations," Stanton said. "It *is* impressive. But I will appreciate it more if you put my mind at ease. Please."

Tattooed jaws stretched. "Right this way, Ambassador."

The Alpha led him along the metal catwalk, which hugged the cavern wall. As they rounded a curvature in the rock, Stanton noticed gravel and tire tracks. *Trucks come down here*, he thought. *To load and unload animals and supplies. There's an exit within reach.*

The Alpha took an unexpected turn, through a narrow opening. Stanton slipped behind him into a pitch-dark passage. The passage wound right, and he stumbled at an unexpected staircase, leading up.

"Watch your step," the Alpha's cold voice echoed.

Stanton climbed the stairs, knees buckling, until he came upon another larger opening, with moon-yellow light. Once again, they had emerged on a metal balcony, fixed to the rock, overlooking an oval-shaped chamber.

A weapons rack lined one wall—shock prods, wrist claws, daggers, swords, and lances. Supply crates were stacked on either side of the room. In the center of the oval, a juvenile *Deinonychus* snarled and approached a frail figure, one of the raiders, a boy with a buzzed head and a sharp black claw tattooed over one eye. He wore combat boots, jeans, and a sleeveless gray undershirt.

"Keep your hands up, boy, or she'll bite 'em off," came a deep, husky voice. The bearded raider Ajax stood on the sidelines, muscular arms folded across his barrel-shaped chest.

Stanton studied the boy more closely. His stomach sank. "Caleb!"

Caleb glanced up and spotted Stanton. The dinosaur snapped at his wrist, and Caleb ducked away defensively, just in time. The animal pounced him. Caleb struggled.

"Let him go!" Stanton shouted. "Please! No!"

"Ambassador." The Alpha placed a hand on his shoulder. "Calm down."

Stanton grabbed the Alpha by the vest. "You psychopaths! You want my help, but you sic a dinosaur on my son?"

The Alpha shoved Stanton. The metal balcony rattled. Then the Alpha pointed down. "Look."

Stanton clutched the metal bars of the catwalk and observed. Ajax hefted the *Deinonychus* off the boy and smacked it on the snout. "Enough, 44!" He turned to Caleb. "*Never* take your eyes off her, boy! Not until you've earned her respect! Do you understand me?"

Caleb nodded. The raider handed Caleb a lumpy gray object: a dead rat. Caleb took a step back, motioned with his hand, and the young *Deinonychus* crouched on her haunches. Caleb held the rat up high. "Stay!" he shouted. "Stay!"

He waited. The *Deinonychus* patiently sat.

Finally, Caleb tossed the rat. "Get it!" The predator snapped it from the air.

"Good girl!" Caleb rubbed the animal's snout and patted her side.

Ajax beamed. "You're a quick learner, kid. But you have a long way to go."

Stanton struggled to his feet. He glared at the Alpha. "What the hell are you doing?"

The Alpha shook his head. "You're unbelievable, Ambassador

Stanton, do you know that?"

"You tattooed my son's face with one of your horrible—" He caught himself. "What is this all about? You're *training* him?"

"This was *your* idea. Your condition was to treat your son as one of my own. Well, here we are."

"I didn't mean for…" Stanton shook his head. "What will people think, eventually, when we go back to Triassica? He's.... *tagged* as one of you."

The Alpha laughed. "If I tried to integrate him with a group of boys his age and he had no ink, he would have been a laughingstock. Now technically, youths have to earn a mark like that, but I'm being very generous, and I'm counting his actions in the supply shed at Columbia as a feat of strength. Your boy catches on fast. I'm actually very impressed with how tough he is… compared to his father."

Stanton fell silent for a moment. "But when we go home, in the end. He's going to be covered in bones and teeth? What will everyone think?"

"Who says he has to go back when it's over? If he likes it here, he can stay."

"I don't want him to stay."

"You wanted him safe. You wanted him to have privileges. This is what it takes here. He has to train and contribute and bond with the animals. And you have my word that as long as we have trust between us, your boy will be one of my pack."

Stanton shook his head. "I just meant for you to treat him well, not make him a..."

"A savage? Does that concern you, Ambassador? Are you afraid that Caleb might like it here?"

Ajax was cornering the juvenile *Deinonychus*, showing Caleb how to corral and disorient the animal. But Caleb's eyes wandered again up to the catwalk. Stanton gave a weak smile and waved. Caleb made no returning gesture. *He's doing what you told him*, Stanton thought. *He's going along with this.*

"You can see more of your son later." The Alpha clapped Stanton's shoulder with tremendous force, and he struggled to remain upright. "You and Caleb will stay here as our guests, for a few weeks. I expect full cooperation."

Stanton nodded. "Yes. Of course."

"You will answer all of my questions about Triassica. You will have limited privileges, but privileges, nonetheless. Caleb will continue to train just as one of our children his age would be required. You will be assigned private quarters with your son and his assigned animal, number 44 down there. I think you will find it to be an upgrade from your previous cell with water."

"Thank you," Stanton said. "I'm glad we reached this understanding."

"Well, I thought about what you said, Ambassador Stanton, and you were right. There is much I can do to motivate you to cooperate. Perhaps in your own way, you might even find a place within our pack. But make no mistake," he lowered his voice, "I have my claws at your son's throat, at all times."

"I understand."

"Good."

Stanton observed as Caleb and Ajax started to train with wooden staffs. The *Deinonychus* lay to the side, head bobbing between them. Ajax shouted words of encouragement as Caleb blocked his every strike.

The Alpha was right. Caleb was good. Living at Columbia, losing his parents, had toughened him. If he was going to convincingly play the part of Caleb's father, Stanton would have to toughen back up too.

You've lived in comfort for too long, Stanton thought. *It's time to go back to your roots.*

8

Stanton battled exhaustion to take as many mental notes as possible about his surroundings. The Alpha led him through many twists in the cave system. Eventually, he lost track of where they were in relation to the holding cell where he had awoken.

First, the Alpha took him to what appeared to be a makeshift infirmary with cabinets and supply drawers. Necra sneered at him, arms folded. "Take your shirt off. Sit." She pointed to a metal table.

Stanton removed his torn jacket and button-down shirt. "*Necra* is your doctor?" He instantly regretted his sarcasm.

The Alpha merely shrugged. "Necra is a highly valued member of our pack. We don't really have doctors per se. We're not that advanced here. Yet."

Necra busied herself, sorting through different colored glass jars. Stanton got a good look at the tattooed *Pteranodon* wings on her back that poked out from behind her tank top. She approached him, digging her fingers into a white paste. "Face the Alpha," she commanded.

Stanton complied, and Necra began to rub the burning paste on the wounds in his back.

"What is that you're applying? Or I'm sorry, am I allowed to ask questions yet?"

The Alpha chuckled. "You can answer that, Necra."

"It is a healing balm. Derived from a plant from the Northern Isles. These wounds are pitiful, but it is a precaution. I see no signs of infection."

"A gesture of good will then," Stanton said. "You trade with Northerners? Or do you steal from them? It seems that you'd need a good relationship with someone for vehicle maintenance and procurement."

"Careful where you fish for information." Necra wiped her hands on her pants and screwed the lid back on her balm. "You might catch a mosasaur."

The Alpha provided Stanton with combat boots, khaki pants, a cotton undershirt, and a leather vest. Then he took him to a cavernous mess hall with rows of wooden tables. Torchlight flickered on the walls. They received food rations at the end of a long line, where raiders stomped, shouted, and made angry demands at a screaming one-eyed woman, covered in piercings. "Line up and shut up, or you get nothing!" She gave a yellow-toothed cackle as she spooned out gruel.

Stanton noted that the Alpha waited in the same line, sat at the same tables, and ate the same food as his subordinates. At the end of the line, the raiders helped themselves to mugs of some kind of beer or mead from a huge wooden cask, but the Alpha himself did not partake, nor did he permit Stanton to indulge. Instead, the Alpha poured Stanton a share of water from his canteen.

Before they sat, the Alpha unclipped a horn from his belt and blew it. It was the same war horn he had heard during the raid on Columbia. Stanton covered his ears.

Memories of racing through the compound flooded over him.

The trashed vehicle.

The pool of blood.

Joe's bitter, broken eyes.

He forced the images back down.

"Listen up!" the Alpha shouted. The hall grew quiet as a crypt. "This here is Ambassador Niles Stanton, from Triassica. He is our guest. You may restrain him if he becomes problematic for any reason, but you are not permitted to harm him. If you have a problem with Ambassador Stanton, you must first see me. Is that clear?"

The crowd grumbled in agreement.

"I want to challenge!" slurred a raspy voice from the front of the food line.

Everyone laughed.

The Alpha smiled. "Grim, you do not want to challenge me today. I will gut you!"

Everyone laughed again.

"I want to challenge!" the man insisted.

The Alpha grinned and shook his head. "Lay off the booze, Grim!"

The crowd cheered.

"All right!" the Alpha shouted. "Let's eat!"

Their meal—Stanton still was not sure yet if this was breakfast, lunch, dinner, or something entirely different—consisted of gray protein paste, a few strips of *Deinonychus* jerky, and a cup of hot broth. The meat was tough and over-salted, the paste practically flavorless, yet still, Stanton eagerly cleaned his plate.

The Alpha took time to savor his food. He did not offer Stanton seconds. Stanton scoured the mess hall but could not find Caleb or Ajax.

Once they both finished, the Alpha presented Stanton with a bronze pocket watch. "Tell time with this. You and your son are sharing quarters. The light goes out at nine p.m. The light comes back on at five a.m., at which time, Caleb reports for training with Ajax."

Stanton opened the pocket watch. It was 6:40 p.m. He let out a long breath. Just knowing the time released a festering knot of anxiety from his chest. *This is a victory,* he thought. *Enjoy it, but don't get cocky. You're still in danger.*

"You were critical of Necra, Ambassador Stanton, but I'm curious: do you yourself have medical training?"

"I meant no offense," Stanton said. "I was surprised that's all. I had assumed she handled the predators based on how we first met."

"We *all* handle the predators," the Alpha said. "Answer the question."

"Basic CPR. No extensive training."

"But if required, you can follow simple directions, correct?"

Stanton hesitated. Nodded.

"Where is the medical facility in Triassica?"

"It's centrally located," he said. "Relatively easy to access, once you're inside the city."

"How are the doctors?"

"They're the best in New Pangea."

"And the nurses? The staff?"

"It's an excellent hospital. They're well-trained. People live long lives inside our walls."

"What kind of training are we talking about, Ambassador Stanton?"

He shook his head, shrugged. "Medical training. I'm not sure I understand this line of questioning."

"Hm." The Alpha rubbed his chin. "No worries. You've had a long day. You've earned some rest."

***

Stanton and Caleb's quarters were another five-by-five-meter room with two hard cots, a low ceiling, and a single fluorescent light. Although the room lacked the support pillar, the chains, and the leaky corner, it wasn't much of an upgrade from Stanton's first cell.

Caleb's *Deinonychus*—number 44—had to sleep in the room with him as part of his training. 44 couldn't have been more than a year old. Standing upright, she came up to Stanton's stomach, and she stretched about two meters in length snout to plumed tail-tip.

The right side of 44's face was missing feathering, and a pale white line slashed the scales on either side of her eye. Her markings mirrored the tattoo that the raiders had given Caleb. Caleb explained it was meant to bond them. 44 had been the runt of her clutch, often attacked by her siblings. She and Caleb both had "uphill battles ahead," according to his trainer Ajax.

After his first day training with the predator, Caleb had scrapes up and down his arms, though no serious wounds. Stanton encouraged him to go along with the training, to accept that it might become increasingly difficult, but to not resist unless he felt his life was in serious danger.

As Caleb talked about his training with Ajax, he absentmindedly fondled the claw tattoo over his eye and rubbed his buzzed hair. Caleb had been issued an oversized khaki vest, jeans, and waterproof combat boots. He had access to certain weapons under Ajax's supervision, but he was not permitted to bring any back to the room.

"You're tough, Caleb, like I said. The Alpha even admitted it to me," Stanton said. "We can survive here. We can figure this out. We'll take it one day at a time."

The boy nodded and yawned. His eyes drooped.

Stanton kept an eye on his watch. Nine p.m. fast approached.

"Always be listening," Stanton told the boy. "Always be absorbing information: about this place, about these people and how life works here. I think our top priority right now, other than keeping our story straight, is to get a strong sense of the geography and layout of this cave system. Do *not* try to escape, but we need to know how the raiders get in and out and how they move supplies in and out. That's our way out, too."

"Not until I get that bull-head man." Caleb lay on his cot.

"Easy," Stanton said. "If we can get him, we will."

The overhead lights shut off, plunging the room into almost total darkness. Soft security lights glowed through the crack under the door.

44 curled up in the corner.

Stanton lay awake processing the day's events. In addition to supplies, the carnivores would need exercise and fresh air. The main predator corrals had to be outdoors, somewhere behind or between the rocky horns that Caleb had described.

Sooner or later, Caleb's training would reveal the location of the carnivore pens. If he couldn't win more of the Alpha's trust, perhaps Caleb could win some from Ajax.

The Alpha was too smart to only have one way in and out, too. There would have to be emergency exits, if not for his men, then at least for himself. Or was he truly as one with his pack as he presented himself? If Triassica or some Northern force ever arrived to end these raiders, would the Alpha stay holed up in his stronghold until the bitter end?

Was he really that kind of leader?

A chill ran down Stanton's spine. Something shifted in the darkness. An inky head bobbed; sharp teeth stretched. 44 was awake, sniffing around. *Is this part of Caleb's training?* he wondered. *Your nocturnal pet—a creature that instinctively wants to gut you— watches as you sleep with one eye open?*

He glanced at the boy's heaving chest on the opposite cot. Caleb was tough, but he did not appear to be sleeping with one eye open.

Sudden weight pressed on Stanton's cot. A long snarl sounded, and hot, foul breath met Stanton's nostrils. He had only taken his eyes off 44 for a moment, and already her jaws were right in his face.

He tensed up, shuffled against the wall. She sniffed his face and neck.

"Get away. Go on..."

44 opened her jaws. Drool dribbled on his chest. Her clawed forearms twitched.

"Go on! Get!"

Get a grip, he thought. *If your fake kid can train a wild animal, then you have to be even* better *at it. Sooner or later, the Alpha will start seriously questioning that you raised him.*

Stanton shoved the *Deinonychus.* She tripped, tore the mattress with her toe claws, and thumped on the ground. She yelped, snarled, then flipped into attack position.

Caleb stirred for a moment, then fell back into a deep snore.

Stanton stood and stared down the animal. He made himself as tall as he could. "Back!" he growled. He held his hands forward.

44 arched the feathers on her back. She snapped and growled.

Stanton recalled the *Troodon* his own father had adopted as a pet. Back before Triassica. When life was simultaneously harder and simpler. *Troodons* were smaller, easier to domesticate if you raised one from an egg, but they could still be dangerous. The *Deinonychus* wasn't so different. Maybe 44 would back down if he smacked her on the snout like he did to his father's pet, Chester.

She lurched forward, jaws open.

Stanton backed away. "You make us sleep with this thing, but don't give us a shock prod, or even a big stick, huh? Very hospitable you piece of—"

44 leapt. She curled her hands around his neck and tackled him to the floor. Stanton struggled, shouted. She snarled and dribbled over his face. Her feathery tail swished the air. Her toe claws prickled Stanton's thighs.

"Get off!" he screamed.

"Hey!" Caleb shouted. "Hey now! Hey!" He appeared over Stanton, arms wrapped around his demented pet's torso. "Easy, girl. Easy, 44. Leave him alone! Lay down! Go!"

The beast wrenched out of Caleb's grip, twisted into the corner, and snapped at the air.

"Hey!" Caleb's voice prickled with exhaustion. He stomped forward and smacked 44's snout. She curled up in a defensive position, tail down, head and neck scrunched between her shoulders. "That's right!" he said. "Lay! Down!"

Stanton shook with rage. "How are we supposed to sleep with that thing trying to kill us?"

Caleb's shadowy form turned to him. "She's not trying to kill us. She was playing with you. She's bored."

"Could have fooled me."

Caleb lowered his voice. "Trust me, *Dad*. If she was trying to kill you, you would be dead."

9

The next morning, as promised, the overhead light blazed to life at five a.m. Ajax was already pounding on their door for Caleb to begin his training. Stanton's joints stiffened. 44 paced the room with hungry eyes.

"Do we get breakfast?" Stanton asked.

Ajax's stormy eyes hardened. "You aren't my priority. I'm to take you to Necra's lab. If she sees fit to feed you, or allow a trip to the mess hall, that's her business."

Ajax permitted them each a chance to use the chamber pot at the end of the stone tunnel, and then led them back into the compound's central hub. Across the main support rock, a large animal snarled. Raiders were shouting. Shock prods sputtered.

"Get back!" one raider announced. "Don't let him touch you, not even a scrape. Don't even let him drool on you!"

The snorts sounded like a *Carnotaurus*, but Stanton knew they weren't poisonous.

"That should hold!" one raider shouted.

"It won't!" another cried.

"Don't tell me how to—" A loud crash echoed. Someone screamed. Wood splintered, and a supply crate tumbled into view.

Ajax held out his arms, blocking Caleb. "Stay back." Ajax unclipped the barbed claws from his belt and secured them over his right wrist, then he readied his shock prod in his other hand.

More shouts and crashes sounded. Two more wooden crates crashed and spilled Columbian iron ore. A huge *Carnotaurus*, back arched, eyes bloodshot, rammed his horned head into view. His round snout opened and unleashed a roar that sounded as much in rage as in pain.

A group of raiders rushed toward the *Carnotaurus* and zapped at his tail and thighs with shock prods. The animal snarled and twisted. His armored tail knocked the raiders onto their backs.

"Stay here!" Ajax marched toward the beast.

Stanton's eyes darted around the cavern, which appeared to him as much a labyrinth today as it had when he first saw it. *If only I had some idea where the exit was,* he thought. *Who knows if there will be another distraction like this.*

"Hey!" Ajax shouted. "You!" He tapped the rocky ground with the tip of his metal shock prod. "That's right, look at me!"

"Ajax, don't!" one of the fallen raiders called.

The bull-head snorted and stared him down. His giant three-toed foot scratched at the spilled ore. He lowered his horns; devilish yellow eyes tilted up in their sockets.

"Come and get me!" Ajax planted himself like a mountain, his muscular arms tensed with readiness.

"Ajax!"

The *Carnotaurus* charged, jaws gnashing.

Stanton grabbed Caleb's arm and whispered. "When I say so,

run." He knew they wouldn't find the way out, but they had an excuse to at least explore without an escort if they were fleeing for their lives.

But in an instant, that excuse vanished. Ajax pivoted, stuck his shock prod under the predator's stumpy arm, and jolted him. The *Carnotaurus* twitched and stumbled. Ajax wasted no time. He stabbed the beast in the soft tissue under his throat and made a long gash all the way to its stomach. Then he yanked the claws free. Blood rained down on him.

The bull collapsed; his eviscerated body thundered against the ground. Ajax wiped his claws on his vest.

"What happened here!" The Alpha rounded the corner, dagger eyes taking in the fallen *Carnotaurus* and the blood-soaked raider.

"Ask them," Ajax said. "They lost control of their animal. We don't let rogue bulls run around. Could have injured people."

"This specimen was not to be harmed!" The Alpha pointed at the dead *Carnotaurus*. He looked Ajax up and down. "You're covered in blood."

"So?"

"So…" The Alpha glanced at Stanton and Caleb. He lowered his voice. "So, wash up. Immediately." The Alpha glanced back at the other raiders who had lost control of their beast. "The rest of you will be disciplined."

The Alpha's face burned crimson with anger, making his tattooed face look even more like the rampaging *Carnotaurus*. He shook his head at the fallen dinosaur. "I wanted this one alive. Get Necra down here right away. You!" He pointed to one of the raiders. "Take Ambassador Stanton to Necra's lab. You! Train the boy."

"*I'm* training the boy," Ajax said.

"You had better go wash up," the Alpha snapped. "You'll take over later. After we have a word. Do I make myself clear?"

Ajax faced down the Alpha for a moment, then stormed back the way they came. Stanton caught his angry glare as they parted out of his way.

***

Stanton waited in Necra's medical lab for close to an hour. By seven a.m., she had returned from the carnivore cleanup in the main hall. "You will facilitate me in organizing and inventorying medical supplies," she explained.

She pointed to several unopened crates, some from Columbia, others from elsewhere. Necra pulled a large binder with yellowing pages from a drawer and slammed it on the counter.

Stanton flipped it open. Handwritten notes filled up the first half of the binder; the rest were blank pages. There were no dates. Items were crossed off. "This is extremely disorganized," he said.

"So, organize it."

"Okay. Why don't we start by going through the cabinet here and sorting through what you have." He opened one door and once again discovered rows of different colored jars and bottles. "Nothing here is labeled. How do you know what's what?"

Necra took a jar out, unscrewed the top and sniffed the contents.

"Aloe balm." She clanked the jar on the counter, then unscrewed another and sniffed. "Fermented honey."

"Fermented honey? Why do you…" Stanton sighed and massaged his temples. "What can I use to label these jars?"

"You are very demanding for a prisoner," Necra said.

"I realize you don't want me in your lab." Stanton made direct eye contact. "But the Alpha has some reason for keeping me here. So why don't we make the most of it."

Necra sneered. "He knows."

"Knows what?"

"How cunning you are. How you push and push for privilege as you poke and prod and hunt for a way out. You will never escape. You will never outsmart him."

Stanton folded his arms. "I consider the Alpha my intellectual equal, in addition to the primary authority here. I understand my situation, and I am cooperating. What more do you ask of me?"

"Know your place," Necra said.

"Do you hate me because I came from the compounds?" Stanton asks. "Or is it because he needs me?"

The *Pteranodon* beak narrowed on her forehead as her eyebrows arched. She whispered, "I could kill you, anytime I want, and he would never, ever know it was me. Organize this shit. I don't care how you do it. Just make sense of it and still your tongue."

10

After Ajax left to scrub himself clean of *Carnotaurus* blood, a thin, quiet raider escorted Caleb and 44 to the training arena. The raider ushered them in and locked the gate behind them.

As the raider turned back down the shadowy cavern, Caleb called out, "Aren't you supposed to train me?"

The raider pointed a saw-edged dagger at Caleb. "You stabbed my brother in the thigh. You're lucky I'm not allowed to kill you." The raider sheathed his dagger and disappeared into darkness.

Caleb smiled as he remembered the raider Whistler from the supply garage in Columbia. *If these psychos can train slashers,* he thought, *so can I.*

Caleb snapped his fingers at 44. He moved his hand back and forth, and she wavered her head to follow his movements. "Are you paying attention," Caleb whispered, "or are you going to try and bite my hand?"

44's gold iris glittered beneath the pale scar that skewered her eye, just like Caleb's tattoo.

"Sit," Caleb tried.

44 snorted. Her lips spread, revealing sharp interlocked teeth.

"Hey." Caleb lowered his hands. The animal craned her neck as he approached her side. Her sickle-shaped toe claws scraped the dusty arena floor. He carefully placed one hand on her neck and the other on her back. "Can you sit for me?"

The feathers on her back bristled. She snarled.

"Come on," he said. "I'm the guy who gives you rats. I just don't have any right this second. Please, sit." He applied pressure to 44's backside.

She snorted, flexed her jaws, and snarled again.

"Fine!" Caleb raised his hands and backed away. "See if you get any rats with that attitude."

Caleb backed toward the far wall. He picked up a handful of rocks and started tossing them at a metal girder fused into the rocky ceiling. Each rock struck the metal with a satisfying *pling!*

44 circled the arena, eyes trained on Caleb. "Are you thinking about eating me?" He lowered his voice. "I've taken down bigger slashers than you, you know." Then he chuckled to himself and repeated the words of the thin raider. "You're lucky I'm not allowed to kill you."

She chirped and cocked her head expectantly.

"No rats!" Caleb snapped. "I know this is the room where you get rats, but we're out of luck. Ajax has the rats. Be patient."

She scratched the dirt, lowered her body, and curled up on the ground.

Caleb sighed. "Now you sit?"

Her tail feathers swished lines in the dust.

Caleb crossed the arena and examined rows of weapons behind a locked gate. Without supervision, he had a chance to take inventory. An electronic keypad secured the arsenal of claws, blades, sticks, and staffs. *No shock prods,* he thought. *They must keep those somewhere else.*

His heart leapt when he spotted an iron blade with a tyrannosaur bone handle—his father's hunting knife. He gritted his teeth.

Stay calm, he thought. *They put that in there to mess with you. Just ignore it. You'll get it back before this is all done…*

The main gate unlocked. Caleb glanced over to find Ajax, in a new vest and pants, beard and hair wet, but clean, eyes harsh as stone.

44 leapt to her feet.

"Get over here, kid," Ajax growled.

Caleb approached.

Ajax nodded toward his side, where two small rodents dangled from his clenched fist. "Give her these. Then follow me. We're taking an excursion."

Caleb took the rodents by the tails and approached the center of the arena. 44 trotted toward him, and he halted her with one hand. She waited. Drool dribbled from her lower lip. He tossed a rodent into the air.

44's gold eyes followed the rat's arc, and she snapped it up in one bite.

"What kind of excursion?" He held his free hand out, and 44 remained still.

"You'll see," Ajax said. "I was planning on training in the arena all week, but it's stuffy down here lately."

Caleb tossed the second rat, and 44 snapped forward. Tiny bones crunched as she guzzled it down.

"Let's hit the road." Ajax's hulking shadow marched down the stone tunnel. Caleb and 44 followed into the main chamber. Three raiders were still scrubbing blood and entrails off the cavern floor, but the bull-head's carcass had been moved.

Ajax rounded the huge stone pillar in the opposite direction of their sleeping chamber. Caleb studied the supply crates stacked against the far side of the pillar. His blood boiled every time he saw symbols for Columbia or Triassica. *That's our stuff,* he thought. *Stolen by you killers.*

The chamber wound into a wide-mouthed opening with metal scaffolding that slanted upward. Blue lights lined the walls. Caleb's stomach fluttered. *It's the way up. The way out.*

Ajax's boots clanked up the walkway. 44 paused, hesitantly testing the metal ramp.

"Don't like that floor, huh?" Caleb asked.

"She'll follow," Ajax assured from above.

44 snarled disapprovingly at the metal grooves. Then she got down on all fours and started to climb the scaffolding as if it were a vertical cliff. They reached another level with more supply crates.

Forklifts were hooked up to chargers in one corner. An elevator platform, big enough for two of the raiders' freight trucks, filled the far side of the cavern. High up, bright, natural light illuminated the red bands of the cavern ceiling.

"Are we leaving?" Caleb asked.

"That's what an excursion is, genius." Ajax approached a cabinet near a metal staircase that led to the top of the elevator shaft. He tapped a code onto a keypad, and the cabinet clicked. Ajax opened it and grabbed a small gun, a wrist claw, and a set of keys, then he shut and secured the cabinet.

Car keys. Caleb followed as Ajax stomped up the metal stairs. They reached the top, and Caleb jumped with surprise as 44 leapt up top and climbed over the metal railing.

Ajax smiled. "You'll get used to her."

Caleb shrugged.

Ajax turned to another keypad. He blocked the buttons with his girth and tapped out another code, then the door unlocked. He led Caleb through. Fresh air wafted over them. Caleb inhaled a deep, satisfying breath. Huge, thick bars and a network of machinery lined the ceiling.

"Panic gates," Caleb said. "Like the ones in Columbia's mines. They keep large predators out."

"Or in." Ajax guided Caleb into bright sun. UV light stung his eyes. Rock-red cliffs glowed into focus. Not a single cloud polluted the azure sky.

Caleb squinted and sighed. A weight lifted off him as he inhaled.

"What's with you?" Ajax asked.

"Nothing just… the sun. The sky. How do you guys stand being down there all the time?"

"Who says we're down there all the time?"

"That's right, I forgot," Caleb said. "You come up to steal and kill people."

"To hunt and gather." Ajax headed down a gravelly path.

Caleb took in his surroundings. Piles of boulders formed a V-shaped wall between devil-horn plateaus. Up close, Caleb could appreciate just how enormous the formations were. It was easily three kilometers to the twin peaks.

At the base of the stone towers were rows of tents and lines of vehicles where raiders performed maintenance. Through a short tunnel to the other side of the rock wall, raiders were training and monitoring *Carnotauruses* and *Deinonychuses* in fenced in areas. High above, Caleb heard the echo of *Pteranodon* cries.

"Truth be told, kid, we're actually underground very little. Mostly to sleep, or train. Always to eat, of course. This clearing is a ghost town when that dinner horn blows." Ajax nodded to some of the other raiders as he passed. They stared curiously at Caleb and 44.

"You supposed to be out here with that kid?" one raider asked.

"You want to eat pachy tonight?" Ajax asked.

The raider chuckled. "Yeah."

"Then don't worry about it."

Ajax approached a rusty, brown jeep. The number three was sprayed on the side. An equally rusted flatbed was hitched behind the jeep—big enough Caleb, realized, for a dead *Pachy-cephalosaurus*. "Hop in." Ajax climbed into the driver's seat.

Caleb got into the passenger seat and 44 leapt in on top of him. "Hey!" He shoved 44, and she snapped at him. "Move! Come on."

Ajax laughed.

"Dinosaurs in the back!" Caleb shouted. "Move it!"

"She can't perch in the back. She'll freak and jump off."

"Well, she's not sitting next to me."

"Yes, she is. You're both runts. You'll fit."

Caleb glared at Ajax, then at the snarling, feathery face wedged next to him. He shuffled left in his seat, and 44 hunkered beside him. Caleb wriggled his arm free and hooked it over 44's back.

"Think of it as quality bonding time." Ajax turned the ignition. The solar engine hummed. He pulled back and peeled away from the lot of vehicles. The flatbed kicked up a cloud of dust.

44 snarled as Caleb struggled to get comfortable. He glanced at the keychain dangling from the dashboard and saw the number three. *If I can get the code for that cabinet, and that security door,* Caleb thought, *we have our way out.*

Caleb twisted in his seat to get his bearings. The flat-tipped horns of the raiders' stronghold shrank into the distance as they drove down the winding road. 44 gnawed Caleb's shoulder.

"Ow!" He forced the dinosaur's head down with both hands. "Enough! Settle down!"

"Don't treat her that way." Ajax popped a cigarette into his mouth and held the wheel with one hand as he positioned a lighter.

"You told me to always be dominant."

"You have to understand her too." He inhaled and puffed gray smoke that spilled in the wind. "You're moving your arm against the grain of her feathering. Always stroke gently from neck to back."

Caleb repositioned his arm, rested it so that his hand touched the nape of 44's neck. Then he slowly stroked downward. Almost instantly, the *Deinonychus* purred and slunk lower.

"So," Caleb asked. "We're hunting pachys? Do you tame them,

too?"

"No sense in that," Ajax said. "They don't listen. We just eat them." The car rumbled off-road. The maroon ridges of the badlands loomed on the horizon.

"You guys don't have pulse tech," Caleb said. "So what's the gun, an air tranq?"

"Mmm-hmm." Ajax puffed his cigarette.

"Do I get a weapon?"

Ajax nodded. "44 is your weapon."

44's gold eye relaxed. She sank into the passenger seat. Her legs and arms folded underneath her. Caleb continued to stroke her neck feathers as he readjusted himself in the seat. He watched a pair of gray *Pteranodons* circling a distant tree. *Something dead over there,* he thought. *Or dying.*

"Is this jeep stolen?" Caleb asked.

"We don't steal everything," Ajax said. "We build. We trade with Northerners."

"But this jeep is stolen, right?" Caleb asked.

Ajax chuckled. "I assume it was, yeah."

"Whose was it?"

"How the hell should I know?"

Caleb shook his head. He glanced back at the distant tree. The pterosaurs had landed, and one was picking at something.

"Listen, kid. You and I are stuck with one another. You and your dad are in a bad situation, and I get that. But we each have a job to do, so let's make the most of it. It's not going to hurt you to train. Your dad cooperates with the Alpha, and the two of you go back to

Triassica. Relax. I'm not your enemy."

"Your people killed my people," Caleb said.

"Listen," Ajax said. "I swear to you, I personally have never led a raid to the mining town. And you, personally, are just the Ambassador's son, right?"

Caleb gritted his teeth and nodded. 44's snout shifted in his lap, and she started kneading the seat with her toe claws. Upholstery shredded.

"Then we're both uninvolved. I never killed your people. Let your dad and the Alpha hash out their business. Just listen and learn, and we'll get along great."

"Why is he the leader?" Caleb asked.

"The Alpha?"

Caleb nodded.

"Because he asserted dominance."

"He's the toughest."

Ajax laughed. He took a long drag and flicked his cigarette into the desert. "He's the toughest one who *wanted* the job."

"You don't want that job, huh?"

"You ask a lot of questions. That's good. That's how you'll learn." Ajax smiled, eyes on the road. "But if you have a question, you ask *me*. Not the Alpha. Not anyone else. Understood?"

"And you'll answer? Truthfully?"

"To a point." He lit a fresh cigarette. "But you're not getting that exit code. And if you're thinking about bolting today, good luck making it from the heart of the badlands back to Columbia, even with my canteen and tranq gun."

"I'm not stupid," Caleb said. Then he added. "And I'm not leaving my dad with you people."

"Do people keep pets in the compounds?" Ajax asked.

"Yeah," Caleb said. "Little ones only, though. They have a zoo too in Triassica."

"You mean 'we,'" Ajax said. "You said '*They* have a zoo.'"

"It's not my zoo." Caleb rolled his eyes. "It belongs to the compound."

"You go to the zoo often?"

"No." *Stop asking about Triassica,* Caleb thought. *I haven't been there for six years.*

"They keep *Deinonychus* there?"

Caleb shrugged. "It's not a big zoo. There's a *Quetzalcoatlus.*"

Ajax whistled. "A huge flyer like that? All by her lonesome, in a cage? That's cruel."

"You care a lot about the zoo."

"I'm just trying to figure something out," Ajax said. "You're good with 44. Damn good. Like you've spent time with her kind. I didn't think they kept predators that size inside the compounds."

Caleb stared forward. 44 purred.

"I guess you're just a natural."

They drove in silence. The sun climbed higher as they swerved between red ridges. The ground grew uneven, and finally Ajax parked the jeep behind a spire of jagged rock. 44 perked up and stretched her toothy jaws with a yawn.

Ajax grinned. "Let's hunt."

II

Ajax climbed out of the jeep and strapped the tranq gun over his shoulder. "We go on foot from here. Pachys like to forage in a creek that cuts through the canyon. Lots of green down there. Watch your footing, though. Wouldn't want to step on a wasp nest."

Caleb reached over 44 and opened the passenger door. She perched on the edge of the seat and leapt onto the dusty ground. Caleb hopped down after her and followed Ajax up a rocky slope.

He turned to find 44 sniffing the air and clawing at a chrome dragonfly dancing in the brush. "Hey!" Caleb snapped his fingers. "Come on! This way!"

"She'll find us," Ajax called.

"Whatever." Caleb hurried up the path. The incline steepened. At several points, Ajax used natural hand and footholds in near vertical inclines to pull himself to the next level. Caleb was sweating by the time he surmounted the third tier of rock. He glanced down to find the jeep was now a good thirty meters below them. 44 had disappeared.

Caleb wiped sweat off his brow. "My slasher ran away."

"No, she didn't." Ajax pushed aside thorny brambles and passed through. Sharp interlocking twigs snapped back into place as he disappeared between red boulders toward the other side of the cliff.

"Couldn't have held those open for me, huh?" Caleb huffed, covered his eyes, and squeezed between jagged twigs. Sharp sticks scraped his bare arms. He popped out the other side. The back of Ajax's toothy tattooed head gleamed in the sun. Caleb took a few steps, and 44 dropped between them.

Caleb's heart skipped a beat. He instinctively shrank into a defensive position.

44 uttered a friendly chirp.

"Told you she'd find us."

Caleb shook his head at the feathery dinosaur and joined Ajax at the cliffside. The view of the canyon stood in stark contrast to the surrounding badlands. Pine trees and vegetation hugged the cliffs. Tall minty grass rolled in the breeze, and a winding river sparkled diamond blue in midday sun. Caleb gave a low whistle. "I didn't think there was anything like this out here."

"Your people just don't know where to look," Ajax said. "The badlands ain't all bad." Then Ajax turned his hardened eyes directly on Caleb. "Remember, watch your step." Ajax started to descend into the trees.

Caleb followed. All around them, insects droned and lazy amphibians croaked. 44's eyes hungrily tracked colorful, blue-tailed *Avisauruses* as they flitted between trees on velvety black wings.

"We're here for a Pachy, but keep your eyes open," Ajax said. "You see a turtle or a big lizard, grab it. Give 44 a piece; don't let her have anything she can't swallow whole."

"How are we going to get the Pachy back up the cliff?" Caleb said.

"Muscle. And rope."

They emerged from the trees. The ground sloped downward and evened out. Waves of tall grass undulated hypnotically as the wind picked up. The pleasant gurgle of the river drew closer.

Ajax held up his hand, then pointed to a game trail where the grass had been matted down by heavy, three-toed footprints.

"Tall grass makes me nervous," Caleb whispered.

"I've never seen anything bigger than a *Deinonychus* down here, kid," Ajax said. "Besides, 44 isn't nervous."

Caleb studied the animal's regal snout bobbing, arms hung low in front of her body, tail a perfectly balanced rod behind her.

"When your animal freaks out, that's when you're in trouble," Ajax explained.

"Other predators could sneak up on her," Caleb said. "Always something worse lurking in New Pangea. That's what my—" Caleb caught himself. "My uncle used to say."

Caleb wasn't sure if that was the kind of expression Ambassador Stanton would use or not, but why risk it?

"Worst things down here are banana-size wasps that sting like holy hell," Ajax whispered. "I'd rather go toe to toe with a T. rex."

Caleb scoured the ground for insect nests. He thought back to Ajax gutting the rogue bull-head under the mountain that morning. *If there ever was a guy who could beat up a rex, it might be you, Ajax.*

They emerged to short grass and the murky shores of the river. Ajax strode right into the water up to his ankles. "Your boots are waterproof, high quality stuff from the islands."

Caleb followed Ajax. The water came up to just below his knees. 44 lowered her head and lapped at the running water. Caleb's tongue felt heavy and dry. He cupped his hand and reached down, but Ajax grabbed his wrist and stopped him.

"It's probably clean enough in a pinch, kid, but don't risk the cholera. You don't have 44's antibodies." Ajax handed him his canteen. They each took a swig.

They continued downstream. The canyon walls towered around them. Somewhere beyond the tall grass, the guttural bleating of a Pachy sounded. "What do you know about them, kid?" Ajax asked.

"Pachys? They're aggressive. Territorial. Plant eaters mostly, but they'll ram you if you get close. We don't see much of them in Columbia, aren't any down by Triassica, but I've eaten them. Kinda gamey." A smug smile crossed Caleb's face. *That's what a compound brat would say, right?*

"They taste a lot better than retired *Carnotaurus* jerky. And you're right to keep your distance. 44 will stay nice and low. Follow her lead when we spot one."

Despite the cool running water around his ankles, Caleb found himself sweating again. Humidity hung in the air. A swampy stench sank around them the further they hiked toward the center of the canyon.

At one point, 44 halted and splashed her face into the river. She plucked out a squirming fish. Its emerald scales glistened in sunlight.

"Get it!" Ajax shouted. "Go on, kid!"

Caleb stumbled waist deep in the river. "Let go!" he commanded. He reached for the fish, and 44 twisted away. Blood and water sprayed with her movements. She chomped, once, twice. Half a fish, still squirming, remained in her claws.

"Give that to me!" Caleb reached, and 44 snapped at him. He tripped onto his back. River water poured over him. 44 gulped down the other half of her fish and gave a sharp smile, red with fish blood.

Ajax laughed. "I told you, don't let her hog a catch she can't swallow in onc bite."

Caleb rose to his feet, face burning red. "I tried! She was too fast! And she doesn't respect me!"

"And she won't if you let her do anything she wants. Next time." Ajax continued downriver.

Caleb leaned close to 44. "Do that again, and I don't care about this stupid training, I *will* kill you. Understand?"

44 chirped and cocked her head. Her eyes glittered. She craned her neck beneath his arm.

Caleb shoved her head away. "No petting!" He splashed back toward the shallow end of the river and muttered. "Dumb animal."

As they marched along, a black and cobalt shape vibrated past Caleb's ear. An enormous wasp landed on Ajax's bicep. The hulking raider froze. He gave a slow half-turn, locked eyes with

Caleb and nodded at the insect as it crawled down his stone-stiff arm on long spidery legs.

"See what I mean?" Ajax said. The blue wasp rubbed spiny forelegs. Tan wings flexed. "Don't move a muscle if one lands on you," Ajax explained. "Just wait for it to leave."

Water sloshed around Caleb's ankles as he approached for a closer look. Charcoal antennae curled from the wasp's bulging red eyes.

"And like I said," Ajax whispered, "if you step on a nest, you're basically fu—"

Caleb snatched the wasp, thorax in one hand, head in the other. In one fluid motion, he twisted it apart. The two halves wriggled. A stinger, with the girth of a carpenter's nail, stabbed uselessly at air outside Caleb's clenched fist.

"Sometimes, when I'm *really* hungry," Caleb said. "I eat one of these." He tossed the two halves into the water. 44 splashed toward the head and gobbled it up.

Ajax's eyes narrowed above his fiery beard. His muscular arms tensed. "Lucky you I didn't get stung." Then he belted out a hearty laugh and clapped Caleb's shoulder with the force of a freighter. "Maybe you *should* have a weapon!"

They hiked onward. The shallow stream emptied by a sandy shore that bled into a dense marsh, packed with fronds and cattails. Ajax motioned for Caleb and 44 to hold back as he surveyed the terrain.

From their new position, Caleb could see far behind them. The canyon cliffs rose high above ridges of pine trees. A white waterfall spilled down one peak, where Caleb imagined the stream began. Near the falls, a gray-backed *Pteranodon* nested. Its pointy beak scanned the treetops.

"All right, kid," Ajax beckoned Caleb to the edge of a line of tall grass. "We're in luck." He pointed out a gold and orange striped *Pachycephalosaurus* wading into the water past a slew of boulders. The Pachy approached the marsh on two legs, then got down on his forearms for a drink. He craned his dome-shaped head and crown of thorns to the rippling surface and lapped water into his hooked beak.

"Sometimes you catch one getting a drink like this," Ajax said. "I'll need to get closer." He readied the tranq gun. "Stay right here. Keep 44 calm."

44 chittered at the sound of her name.

Ajax rounded the brush and crept low. He kept left of the boulders, blocking himself from the Pachy's line of sight. Caleb stroked 44's feathery neck. *I should have let you get stung, Ajax*, he thought.

Columbians called the wasps "Lizard Hawks" because the females laid eggs inside small reptiles and dragged them into their burrows. The wasps' young hatched inside the unfortunate lizards and ate their way free.

Just like Caleb had gotten good at picking off *Deinonychus*, he'd gotten good at snatching big, scary-looking bugs out of the air too. All the kids in Columbia were good at that. When raiders stole your rations, you had to eat something.

Caleb's eyes drifted away from the creeping raider, toward the golden-domed dinosaur drinking peacefully. Midday sun shimmered across rippling water. A breeze carried through the canyon and ruffled the cattails.

For a moment, Caleb spotted something.

He gasped. His hand squeezed the scruff at the base of 44's neck, and she chirped with surprise.

He kept his eyes focused on that same spot. The cattails shifted again. A large, two-legged carnivore crouched in the marsh.

"We're not the only ones hunting Pachys today," Caleb whispered. 44 purred. His father was right. *Always something worse lurking in New Pangea.*

The camouflaged predator was bigger than a slasher, smaller than a bull-head. Maybe six meters long. It was impossible to tell with it blending in and being half-submerged. Caleb didn't know of any color-changers native to the badlands. People spoke of them in lusher areas. "Whatever that is, it came a long way, 44."

Ajax crouched behind the closest boulder. Soon he would be in range of the Pachy—and in reach of the ambush predator.

This is my chance. Caleb's heart pounded. *Let that thing take out Ajax, get his keys, and then get out of here.* True, he didn't know exactly where he was, but if he just drove east, sooner or later he'd reach Columbia or the road to Triassica. *Just follow the sunrise.*

Ajax gave Caleb a salute. He stealthily rounded the first boulder and hid again.

He hasn't noticed it, he thought. *He's only thinking about the Pachy. For all his tough guy act, he's just another dumb raider. He deserves to be ripped apart. They all do.*

Then Caleb thought about the man with the *Carnotaurus* face.

That's who he really wanted to see ripped apart.

And even if he did drive east, then what?

Ambassador Stanton would die for sure.

The raiders would come back to Columbia.

When the Pachy dipped down for another drink, Ajax crept closer. He raised the tranq gun.

"Ajax stop!" Caleb's voice echoed.

The Pachy perked up and bleated with alarm. Ajax cursed in frustration. He fired, just as an enormous rush of water pushed toward shore. The Pachy wheeled around; the dart whizzed past his orange striped shoulders.

The camouflaged predator surged forward. His tan and brown skin finally contrasted against the water.

The dinosaur resembled a predator like a T. rex, but smaller, with a narrower snout and longer, three-fingered arms. Caleb struggled to come up with the name. *Starts with a D...*

The Pachy scrambled to shore. The predator snapped at the fleeing prey's tail and snarled. Ajax rolled back behind the boulder and froze against it. He shook his head at Caleb and motioned for him to stay hidden.

Back on land, the Pachy whirled around and charged the bigger dinosaur. His spiky head collided with the predator's side. The predator grunted with pain at first, but then he snatched the Pachy's neck and bit hard. His pebbly skin started to shift from the browns and tans of the cattails and reeds to a sandy beige.

Dryptosaurus, Caleb at last remembered. *"Invisible Assassins" of the north shores.*

The Pachy cried in pain as the *Dryptosaurus* took a second bite. Neck bones snapped. The Pachy's arms slackened, and the bigger dinosaur shoved him onto the sand. He snorted, sniffed the air, and raised his scaly ridges in Ajax's direction.

Ajax worked to load another tranq dart, but before the shot was ready, the ambush predator was already rounding the boulder.

"Run!" Caleb shouted.

Ajax leapt to his feet and raced to one side. The *Dryptosaurus* turned in Caleb's direction and snarled. 44 chittered with alarm and darted into the tall grass. The predator barreled down on them. Caleb couldn't think of a better plan, so he followed his pet slasher into the brush.

The *Dryptosaurus* splashed in the stream where Caleb had been lurking and unleashed an irritated growl. He stomped into the brush, sniffing and snuffling, clawing tall grass aside in search. Caleb had lost sight of 44—who he knew had better instincts for hiding than he did. The predator's ridged tail swayed in the air.

A high-pitched buzz sounded nearby. Caleb glanced around, and spotted metallic blue bugs crawling between dry fronds, in and out of a dirt mound. He carefully crawled around the vibrating pile. He heard the big dinosaur searching behind him.

"Hey come on! Over here!" A booming voice called out. Ajax was trying to lure the predator back toward the shore, away from Caleb.

But the dinosaur seemed only interested in the smaller, tastier morsels in the tall grass.

Caleb rounded the wasp mound. The dryptosaur's crocodilian snout drew closer. Large three-fingered hands raked the grass.

"Hey!" Caleb popped to his feet and waved his arms. "Over here, ugly!"

"Kid! No!" Ajax shouted.

The dryptosaur's scales had turned pale green to match the tall grass. He opened his mouth wide and lurched forward. Caleb dove for the sandy clearing. Ajax was rushing forward, tranq ready.

The dinosaur roared with pain as his three-toed foot came down on the wasp mound. Black and blue insects swarmed. One landed on the dinosaur's snout and stung his big, yellow eye.

"Get behind me!" Ajax pushed Caleb aside. "Head for cover!"

Caleb lingered and watched as Ajax fired a tranq at the color-changer's neck. The tip of the needle broke against the predator's hard skull. He lumbered out of the brush on muscular plant-green legs and whipped around to swat more insects.

As Ajax attempted to load another dart, the predator's muscular tail whacked him in the head. The hulking raider fell to one side. Caleb spotted Ajax's wrist claw, strapped to his thigh, just below the jeep keys, which jangled from a clip on his belt. Ajax lay dazed.

The *Dryptosaurus* roared and snapped until the wasps disbursed.

Caleb raced toward Ajax. He skidded in the sand and reached for the jeep keys.

The predator snarled and snapped downward. Caleb raised his arms in defense.

Suddenly, a high-pitched shriek echoed. 44 leapt into the air, red feathers blazing in the sun. She sank her claws into the larger predator's side. She bit hard into the predator's shoulder and slashed ferociously with her toe claws. The predator spun around and attempted to bite back, but 44 was just out of range.

Caleb quickly worked at the straps on Ajax's leg. He slid the barbed claw out, and hastily strapped it around his wrist, gripping the handle tight.

The *Dryptosaurus* finally managed to grab 44's ankle with one hand and yanked her onto the sand. He pinned her beneath his foot. Swollen red wasp stings showed against shifting green-beige scales.

Caleb dove.

Just as the dryptosaur's head came down, Caleb shot his fist upward, burying the raider claws into the larger dinosaur's neck. Ribbons of blood spurted down as Caleb yanked the claw free from his throat. The dryptosaur choked, gagged. Caleb backed away as the predator took a few listless steps toward the water, then collapsed to one side. His muscular leg twitched. His tail curled into the air, then fell slack.

Blood pooled and seeped into the stream.

Ajax woozily climbed to his feet, rubbing his bruised face. "Sweet holy hellhole, kid," he marveled, wide-eyed at the dead dinosaur, then at the boy covered in blood. "I've never seen a *Dryptosaurus* before. Never *would* have seen it coming if you hadn't…" He shook his head in disbelief.

The dryptosaur's leg finally stopped twitching. His camouflage skin slowly settled to a dull, neutral gray tone.

Caleb struggled to catch his breath. 44 chittered, whimpered, and licked his cheeks. Caleb wrapped his arms around 44's neck and set his forehead against her snout.

A Deinonychus *just saved your life.* The thought echoed. *She* actually *came back for you.*

Ajax clasped Caleb's left hand and hoisted him to his feet.

Caleb held up the claw. "Do I get to have one of these now?"

Ajax slowly nodded. "Yeah. You do. Out here with me at least." He whistled and shouted with triumph. "What do you want for dinner kid? Pachy or *Dryptosaurus*?"

They worked the rest of that day, carving and hacking off the Pachy's legs and tail.

44 was rewarded with a few choice selections before they wrapped and hoisted what they could carry back upstream and over the canyon wall. They lowered the meat down the steeper sections of the outer cliff and secured them to the flatbed behind Ajax's jeep. It took two trips. The carcasses were messy with flies and beetles by the time they were done. They left the remains for the pterosaurs.

Their arms and 44's snout were stained with dinosaur blood by the time they were done. Caleb's entire body ached, but besting the *Dryptosaurus* left him feeling exhilarated, strangely free—even though he knew he was still the raiders' prisoner.

As they drove back, the sun was getting low. *Pteranodon* calls echoed over the hum of the solar engine. Ajax beamed. "You did good today, kid." He hesitated, nodded. "Better than anyone your age I've ever known. You deserve to know that."

Caleb smiled. "Thanks." 44 nuzzled his arm and rested her head in his lap.

"She's going to respect you from now on too," Ajax assured. "Just wait. You crossed a bridge with her today."

With you too, I hope, Caleb thought. *Because if you trust me to have a weapon, sooner or later I'll be close enough to the Alpha to stick* him *in the throat.* He smiled wider.

"Caleb." Ajax raised an eyebrow. "Just wondering something."

"What?"

"Is it common for a compound brat to be so hungry he has to fry up a desert wasp for dinner?"

Caleb returned Ajax's inquiring glare with confidence. "My dad and I spend a lot of time traveling. When we're in Columbia, we eat what they have. And they don't have a lot."

"Ah." Ajax lit a cigarette with one hand and steered with the other. "That explains it."

Over the horizon, Caleb spotted the rocky horns of the raiders' base glowing in the afternoon sun.

13

Every morning, Stanton continued to report to Necra's lab, where he sorted medication and supplies. Throughout the day, Necra disappeared for odd swaths of time, fifteen minutes here, an hour there. Stanton tried to use that time to inventory useful items he could try and smuggle from the lab—things that could aid an escape.

He didn't dare risk taking anything. Not yet. He couldn't be sure if or when his captors might search his pockets. So far, no such search had occurred.

He had yet to discover any anesthetics strong enough to knock out a guard. Perhaps the raiders were well-acquainted enough with pain that they didn't need it.

Somewhere, there had to be animal tranquilizers—maybe a separate vet lab where they also kept stimulants for their *Carnotaurus* attacks.

When Necra was present, she worked begrudgingly with Stanton to help sort supplies. Stanton noted that several boxes they unloaded contained lab equipment: burners, beakers, and glassware. Necra set these supplies aside to be collected by another raider.

There was definitely a second lab.

When they weren't organizing equipment, Necra treated wounds from the animal handlers, gashes and scrapes mostly.

The injured raiders seemed proud to be there, each of them with a story to tell: "Number 16 gnawed my shoulder when I turned my back." "29 nearly severed my femoral artery!"

As she stitched up her patients, Necra gave tips on *Deinonychus* whispering. "Treat your animal like a lover," she instructed at least three times a day—to which every raider responded with his own uniquely raunchy punchline.

At one point, Stanton found a numbing agent in a box from a Northern city. He suggested it could be used to dull the pain of her needle as she stitched up an injured raider's thigh.

They laughed at him.

"Pain is a teacher," Necra said. "Your lesson is coming."

Necra provided generally good medical advice to her patients, but Stanton could tell she had no formal training. Still, there was something different about her from the other raiders, more than just the slight Northern accent she attempted to hide. She knew a lot about the animals and their biology. She knew a lot about the bottled chemicals and substances and the disorganized lab equipment.

Necra was not a medical doctor, but she was educated—perhaps as a scientist.

Each night, the Alpha dined with Stanton and posed a handful of questions about Triassica. Stanton struggled to make sense of the impending favors. So far, the Alpha's inquiries only suggested a desire for broad knowledge about the compound's infrastructure.

Stanton answered truthfully, confident that he was only giving the Alpha reasons *not* to attempt a raid on such a heavily fortified city. He was eager to see how the line of questioning would develop, but he couldn't guess the specifics of the Alpha's plan.

Every night, in the short hour they had before lights out, Stanton and Caleb searched the cell—in case the raiders should ever decide to bug their beds with a radio transmitter. Then they shared their day's events. Caleb kept Stanton up to date on his training. He described the exit, the industrial elevator that led to the exterior, as well the surrounding landscape. To Stanton's astonishment, in a short time, number 44 became increasingly submissive to Caleb. She slept always at the foot of his bed and only stirred when the boy was awake.

"Ajax says she's at just the right age for imprinting on a person," Caleb explained. He was playing tug of war with an old chew rope that Ajax had given him. 44 snarled and wriggled her feathery tail. "But he said it's still pretty amazing I got her to listen this good, this fast. I guess it's because we saved each other."

"And because you understand her kind," Stanton asked. "You killed… how many?"

"Five. Seven including the two at the supply garage." He tugged 44 close and ruffled her downy forehead. "You were almost eight, girl! I was *this* close!" Caleb pinched his thumb and forefinger centimeters apart.

44 snarled and yanked the rope.

"You didn't tell Ajax any of that, did you? I mean he knows about the two you killed that day, but he doesn't know you had been making sport of it."

Caleb shook his head.

"Good." Stanton locked eyes with him. "Be careful. Don't show off."

"It's a little late for that." Caleb released the chew rope and sat against the wall; 44 curled up next to him and gnawed her rope.

Stanton hoped that Caleb had told him all the relevant details of his Pachy hunt with Ajax. No doubt Ajax was surprised to see a kid from Triassica take down a *Dryptosaurus*. They would have to work hard to sell the narrative of the two of them, frequently on the road, always in danger, living as locals live outside compound walls.

That wasn't totally true of Stanton's job as ambassador, but how would the raiders know?

"Here's the thing," Caleb said. "Ajax respects me now. He might respect me even more if I tell him how many dinosaurs I've killed."

"It wouldn't make sense," Stanton said. "Why would an ambassador's son from Triassica go around hunting dinosaurs in the badlands?"

"We'll say you took me hunting," Caleb said.

"Hunters from the compounds use pulse rifles—not knives, claws, and pickaxes. But you might be onto something. Ajax does seem to like you. And if he *is* suspicious about your upbringing, I don't get the sense he's shared that with the Alpha."

"He's starting to trust me." Caleb fingered the tattered ends of the chew rope dangling from his pet's jaws. "He let me have this rope for 44. I could use this to strangle a guard."

Stanton glared. "Don't."

Caleb grinned.

"And don't push that trust. Let it grow naturally. Maybe down the line we can use that relationship, but we don't have a plan for how or why yet. Other than your one excursion, you still train in that round cave?"

"Yeah," Caleb said. "The arena."

"What about the predator pens? Have you seen them?"

"Briefly. They're around the other side of the horns, through the tunnel under the boulder field. I hear *Carnotauruses* down here sometimes too. I think there are a few smaller pens underground."

"We have too much supervision right now," Stanton said. "But we're getting somewhere. Sooner or later, I'll find out where they keep the animal stimulants they use during their raids. There's a second lab somewhere. Maybe eventually Necra will have me assist her there."

"They've got a pretty good system," Caleb said.

"They're not perfect, Caleb. Look how they leave stolen supplies out like trophies. How they hoard and stockpile. They don't have room to store it all, so the crates sit in the main cavern. They get stacked up in the lab, in the halls. Some of those crates are food and ore. Others have weapons and drugs."

Caleb nodded. 44 lost interest in the chew rope and nuzzled his lap.

"That episode with the rogue *Carnotaurus* proved that the raiders can lose control over their animals. If we can make a distraction—unleash their pets against them—maybe that's our window to escape."

"If we unleash a bunch of rogue bulls," Caleb said, "aren't we in just as much danger?"

"Aren't we already?" Stanton said.

The lights shut down, plunging them into darkness.

14

The next day, the Alpha and Stanton dined in the mess hall. Once again, the raiders were crowded around the mead casks, but the Alpha did not partake.

Chemical dependency, Stanton thought. *The mead helps him control the pack. A daily reward of alcohol in the mess hall keeps his soldiers happy. Makes them agreeable. Encourages them to be fearless.*

When they sat, Stanton spotted hulking, red-bearded Ajax with Caleb trailing him in the food line. It had been the first time in a while that their meals intersected, and Stanton couldn't help but think there must be something deliberate about that.

The Alpha's tattooed smile beamed from across the table.

Stanton smiled politely in return.

"Tell me about the plumbing," the Alpha said.

"In Triassica? It's advanced. Everyone has running water, toilets. That's not uncommon in the south, you know. Even small towns and settlements—"

"Don't be a prick, Ambassador. I know we have well-water and chamber pots here, but there's plumbing in the north too. It's not like you people invented it."

"I wasn't implying—"

"Do you desalinate from the ocean or use groundwater?"

"A little of both," Stanton said.

Ajax and Caleb sat at their table. Ajax nodded in acknowledgement.

"How is my son's training going?" Stanton asked.

Stanton caught a glint in Ajax's smile. Was it pride? "Caleb, tell your father—"

"You boys can chit-chat about training on your own time," the Alpha said.

Ajax shrugged and shoveled food in his mouth. He started to talk to Caleb in hushed tones—something about 44—as the Alpha continued to interrogate.

"Any pest problems? Does the sewage attract," he shrugged, "'dactyls, compies? Anything like that?"

"Sometimes coelophysids make a den that we have to clear out."

The Alpha smiled and nodded. "Slippery little things. Must get in from the marshes, huh? Coelophysids ever attack folk?"

"They don't get that big."

"They bite, though."

"I suppose, now and then, a sewer worker might get bitten." Stanton shrugged.

As the Alpha began another question, a thumping drowned out his words. He glanced back in annoyance.

A few tables down, raiders pounded their fists in unison. Silverware rattled. "That's right! That's right!" A gruff voice slurred. Stanton spotted a familiar drunken raider, swaying toward their table. "That's right, challenge!" He turned to his own table and raised his arms. They pounded louder. "Challenge! Challenge!"

The raiders at the other table started to chant with him, to roar "Challenge! Challenge!" They stomped their feet.

The Alpha stood, folded his arms, and aimed his carnivore smile at the drunk man. "A little early, even for you, isn't it, Grim?"

More tables were pounding now: "Challenge! Challenge! Challenge! Challenge!"

"I just…" Grim approached, grinning and glassy-eyed. He fumbled to unlatch the claw strapped to his thigh, then struggled to strap it to his wrist. "We haven't had a challenge in quite a while, and we was just saying…"

"You don't want to challenge me, Grim. I like you."

"We all like you. It's just…"

"Just the sport of it. You miss it?"

Grim laughed. Shrugged.

The other raiders stomped and pounded.

"How about a friendly spar?" The Alpha suggested. "Later tonight, before lights out. With sticks in the arena, not claws."

Grim swayed and pointed the barbed tips of his claws. "How about, you'd like because—cuz then you stay Alpha…"

The Alpha sighed. "All right, Grim, have it your way. I accept your challenge."

Grim rushed forward and thrust his claw with surprising agility. The Alpha twisted out of the way. In an instant, he had his own wrist claw attached. He snatched Grim by the collar of his jacket and intercepted his clawed fist.

The Alpha cracked Grim's skull against the table.

Ajax, Caleb, and Stanton, all backed away. Blood dripped from Grim's forehead into the protein gruel on the Alpha's lunch tray.

The other raiders pounded and clapped.

Caleb stared, wide-eyed.

Ajax smiled broadly, arms folding again over his muscular chest.

"Yield!" Grim shouted. "I yield! I yield."

"You *can't* yield!" the Alpha snarled. "I gave you the chance to yield, Grim. I entertained your little dream of fighting me practically every night for the past month. You wanted a challenge. Here it is."

The Alpha flipped Grim onto his back, then shoved barbed claws into the man's belly. Grim unleashed a guttural "Ooooooo-ooh." Red liquid dribbled down his chin.

"Sorry, Grim. Wish I could do this to the idiots who put you up to it." He yanked his claws free, tearing stringy entrails with them.

Then, splattered in the dead man's blood, the Alpha raised his arms in victory and turned in a circle to address the room. "Maybe I will do just that. Maybe I'll hunt down the cowards who convinced old Grim here that he was a match for me."

The mess hall grew dead quiet.

The Alpha's muscles tensed, his breathing harshened with bloodlust. Finally, his eyes landed on Stanton. "Care to try your luck, Ambassador Stanton?" he asked. "This is one way out, you know."

15

That night, Stanton and Caleb briskly compared notes before lights-out. Stony unease hung between them in the wake of Grim's death. Stanton lay in darkness, as he had every night, considering the Alpha's motives.

The Alpha killed Grim partly as a reminder to his pack to think twice about challenging. But murdering a sloppy drunk was hardly the most convincing display of dominance for the raiders.

Was it also a message for Stanton? *This is one way out you know.*

Not everything the Alpha does is directed at you, he reminded himself. Still, he couldn't help but feel like every moment of every day under the horns slowly integrated him into the Alpha's plans. Like every supply crate he sorted for Necra held some clue to an impending evil deed.

The next morning, Stanton arrived at the lab to find the tables and counters clean and empty. No crates to sort or unpack. Necra arrived soon after. She beckoned him with a bony finger. "Follow me. I want to show you something."

Stanton had learned by now not to push for more information when one of his captors led him through the cold, confined underground to some mystery location. The raiders had an unspoken rule of *You'll see when we get there*. It was really starting to annoy him.

Necra had been especially intolerant of Stanton's questions or ideas. She assumed his every inquiry to be part of an escape effort. Which, of course, was correct.

She led him through a large manmade opening in the cave system. A hand-painted sign read "Vet Bay." To the right, hulking carnotaurs loomed in cramped, gated cells.

Long metal pins, not locks, secured the gates, Stanton noted. It would be easy to let one loose.

Steel tables, animal handling equipment, and of course the usual haphazard stacks of raider spoils lined the walls, but Stanton didn't see any drugs or tranquilizers out in the open. Steel cabinets and what looked like a large refrigerator occupied one corner.

But Necra swiftly proceeded past the cells of snorting bull-heads into another dim blue hallway that wound leftward.

At least now we know where they keep a few carnotaurs, he thought. Another chunk of the cave system was coming together in his mental map. Necra had to be rounding the circular "horn" shape of the southern mountain.

She stopped at an opening in the rock and pulled a metal lever; accordion gates slid open, exposing a dark shaft with metal beams and cables—an elevator. Stanton followed her onto the elevator. She pulled another lever and the gates slid shut.

As rusty gears cranked them up into darkness, a pit formed in Stanton's stomach. *Of all the raiders, Necra seems to hate me the most, and here I am stuck in the slowest, darkest elevator in New Pangea, crawling my way up to where exactly?*

Light glimmered far above. He couldn't suppress his curiosity any longer. "Are we going all the way to the top?"

"So impatient," Necra said.

"Are you plotting to throw me off the mountain?"

"It's not a mountain," she said. "It's a remarkable geological phenomenon. Mountains are much larger."

"Well, if you're planning to toss me to my death, at least indulge me about what's so remarkable."

Necra sighed. "You must truly love the sound of your own voice, Stanton. You struggle to keep your mouth shut, but inevitably, you inundate me with snide comments and disrespect."

The light grew brighter. They were approaching a makeshift roof of some kind. Necra gave a sickly-sweet smile. "Nothing to say to that?"

"Conversation is in my nature."

"We know." At last, the elevator halted at the top. A breeze shuddered the tin roof. Stanton's eyes stung at the influx of natural light. The sapphire sky seemed a mirage at first. He took a long, precious breath.

I've been underground for so long, he realized. *So focused on survival that I hardly realized how much I craved this.* The visual splendor of sky, blazing yellow sun, precious air, the rocky gray edges of the twin peak, and deep maroon cliffs—it all seemed to sing through his bones. A feeling of openness, of freedom oozed inside him.

He took cautious steps out of the shaft onto the flat plateau of the horn. He turned and marveled at the panoramic view of open desert and distant badlands. The practically identical twin horn stood across a great chasm. Its gray-black striations glistened in sunlight.

Far below, a wall of boulders piled high over a manmade access tunnel that led to the northern side of the horns, where metal fencing formed two spacious pens, built against the rock. A gray lookout tower stretched above the opposite horn. A raider sat in the crow's nest, binoculars hanging from his neck.

Solar panels lined the lookout tower, and two large cylindrical generators stood on either end of the eastern horn. Stanton turned to find rows of mismatched solar paneling set up along the inner circle of the western horn where he stood. Old models, but effective. The cabling was bolted into the stone. It snaked in a semi-circle and tucked down into the edges of the elevator shaft, presumably to some generator-filled cavern that powered half the raiders' operation.

Stanton sucked in breaths of fresh air like a man who had been seconds away from drowning. "Well," he said. "If you are going to kill me, thank you for doing it outside."

Necra pushed past him and walked toward a rocky platform. High above, shadowy *Pteranodons* circled. She cupped her hands over her mouth and let out a long, high-pitched shriek, a near perfect pterosaur call.

Then she faced Stanton. She spread her arms like a priestess. Her dark eyes gleamed on either side of her tattooed beak. "I told you already, Ambassador. If I want to kill you, you won't be able to stop me—and you won't expect it."

An enormous *Pteranodon* thundered down behind her. Dust puffed around them, like magic powder. The pterosaur let out a hungry squeal and craned the arrow of his face over Necra's shoulder. She caressed his leathery neck as wings folded around her like an enormous gray blanket.

Stanton's jaw dropped. *That explains her tattoos.*

"You're surprised by this?"

"I've never, *ever* heard of anyone training a pterosaur, let alone a big one," Stanton said. "I'm impressed, but not surprised. I've come to respect your people's rapport with animals."

Necra glared.

"Learn to take a compliment, Necra."

"The raiders did not train *Pteranodons* until I showed them it could be done." She reached into a pouch on her belt and fed a tiny rodent to the affectionate flyer. "They cannot be used for hunting, not really, but I studied their migratory patterns. We've altered their flight paths."

Necra stooped and tended to something on the *Pteranodon's* leg, a leather strap. Stanton watched carefully. When the pterosaur stretched his wings, he noticed Necra unstrapping a burlap scroll.

"You use them as messengers. To where? A western camp?" Stanton continued to survey their surroundings. To the south, he spotted scores of vehicles—jeeps, trailers, and quad bikes. The layout perfectly matched Caleb's descriptions. A structure hugged part of the eastern horn as well, some kind of garage.

"We don't *use* the pterosaurs." Necra stowed the message in her pocket and fed her pet another mouse. "It's symbiosis. They get food; we get messages."

"I've noticed that Caleb is the only child here," Stanton said. "I assume the children are trained in a western settlement, then? Is that why there are so few women here as well? Are they held there?"

"*Held* there?" Necra scoffed. "So ignorant!"

"So, educate me," Stanton snapped. "You make me stand around and guess, and then have an attitude that I'm ignorant. My son is being trained as one of you, and you don't think I want to understand?" Stanton moved closer. "Help me understand."

The pterosaur snapped. Stanton flinched and stepped back.

Necra gave her pet a soothing whisper and stepped out from behind his wing. "Why do you think I have taken you up here today?"

"I assume to threaten me." Stanton allowed the anger to seep into his words. "So go ahead, play more games, while I wonder and worry about my son."

Necra reached into another pocket and pulled out a strip of animal jerky. She tore it and offered half to Stanton. "The Alpha has ordered me to bond with you."

Stanton pondered if that was good or bad. The truth or a lie. He eyed the jerky with suspicion.

"It's not poison." Necra bit her own piece. "See?"

He accepted the jerky.

"This meat is from the dryptosaur that your son slaughtered. Ajax speaks highly of Caleb. You are free now to ask questions about your son's training."

"Caleb tells me everything about his training," Stanton said. "So far, he speaks highly of Ajax too. I appreciate the degree of respect that my son has received."

Necra circled the rim of the horn. Her *Pteranodon* folded up his wings and crawled behind her on stubby claws. "You are partially correct about the western camp. That is where we train our young. There are many women there, but I resent your insinuation that they are captives."

"I apologize." Stanton kept his distance and followed Necra. Her *Pteranodon* stole threatening backward glances as he stalked along, head and wings all folded triangles and sharp cones. The flyer looked even stranger on land than in the sky.

"I was not born a raider, as I'm sure you've guessed," Necra said. "I'm from a north island called Cambria. My father was a wealthy man there. A scholar and a doctor. He taught me everything that I know about animals and medicine."

What should I say to that? Stanton wondered. *That her father would be proud? Somehow, I doubt that.*

Necra continued, "My father knew I was bright. He encouraged me to read and cherish knowledge. He brought me to the hospital where he worked and boasted of his 'little learner' to his colleagues.

"But when I came of age, his doting ways melted like a castle of sand in ocean surf. He made a pact with another family to ensure our wealth." She paused and took a moment to affectionately stroke her pterosaur's beak. She slipped the creature another mouse.

"An arranged marriage?" Stanton guessed. "I've heard that's common among privileged classes in the North."

"I was fourteen, Ambassador Stanton, not much older than your son, being forced into the bed of a much older man. I ask you: is that privilege?"

"It is not," Stanton agreed.

"I begged my father to call off the wedding. 'You'll understand in time, pet,' he assured me. We arrived by ship the week of the ceremony, and by the mercy of fate, *they* arrived that same morning. Their war horn echoed across the harbor."

"Raiders," Stanton whispered.

A blissful smile spread as Necra surveyed the land below them. Stanton glanced down and spotted a large, fenced-in area where raiders worked with full-grown *Deinonychuses*.

"I was afraid at first," Necra said. "The attack happened quickly. The pack of raiders had hijacked a medium-sized vessel, a freighter from the western shore. They had no advanced weaponry, but they had the element of surprise, and fifteen *Deinonychuses* stowed below deck.

"Within minutes, they slaughtered the dock workers with a barrage of arrows and a firebomb. It was pure luck that we were on the pier that day to meet my betrothed, a fat, forty-year-old covered in warts. He looked like a pincushion by the time it was over." She laughed.

"My father ordered our crew to turn back, but a *Deinonychus* leapt from the pier onto our vessel. I hid below deck and listened to the horns. The snarls and growls." She sighed. The *Pteranodon* crooned at her touch.

"That's a nightmare, especially for a young person," Stanton said.

"At first, it was," Necra said dreamily. She walked away from the edge, toward the center of the plateau. Her *Pteranodon* dutifully followed the wings on her tattooed back. "Then I emerged. The raiders had already boarded our vessel. They were already looting. We had no weapons, but we did have precious metals, Northern currency in large amounts, silks and other goods, meant as gifts for my new family.

"I saw him for the first time, and I was not afraid. He had horns tattooed over his eyes, but at that time, no inked teeth. A line of hair, then, like a *Spinosaurus* sail, traced his scalp." She ran her fingers through her black mohawk.

The Alpha, Stanton thought. *In his younger years.*

"Around him, the crew lay in blood. Dinosaurs picked at them. He told me not to look, but I *wanted* to look. I wanted to see all of it. He told me that they did not wish to hurt me, and that they would take me back to shore. They only wanted the valuables."

Pteranodon cries echoed above the horns. Necra's pet pointed its face skyward.

"You didn't go back to shore though, did you?" Stanton asked.

"No." She smiled. "I laughed at them. I told them that they were stupid. The man who would one day become Alpha smiled at me. He asked why I thought that. And I told him that silks and coins were worthless. The treasure was below deck."

Stanton shook his head in confusion. "Solar cells? Weapons?"

"Books, Ambassador Stanton. Knowledge. My father brought a library of scientific tomes wherever we went, containing knowledge passed down from the earliest humans who settled New Pangea. It is literature that taught me techniques to tame this creature." She stroked the pterosaur's neck. "Up until then, the raiders had only harnessed *Deinonychus*. They had only the western camp. They had much to learn."

"You had much to teach," Stanton said.

Necra nodded. "And now the Alpha wishes to learn from *you*."

Is that the reason for Necra's special bitterness toward me? Stanton wondered. *Jealousy?*

"Your father was a victim," Stanton said.

Necra's nostalgic grin faded. "My father was vile. Willing to sacrifice his child for a pile of coins. He was weak. His was stupid. The raiders do not see women this way."

"Tell that to the women murdered in Columbia," Stanton said.

She scowled. "Our people are not rapists."

"I will take your word for that." Stanton shrugged. "They *are* murderers."

"We are liberators!" she shouted. "The most glorious sight of my life was hours after the raid that freed me. The raiders had secured three vessels and loaded them with supplies. I had agreed to join them. And as we sailed away, I watched these glorious, beautiful creatures," she stroked her *Pteranodon's* beak, "descend upon that pier to scavenge what we left behind, and I instantly loved them."

Her *Pteranodon* lowered his head, and she kissed the tip of his gray crest. "I watched what remained of my father sink into red water that day. I never wanted to belong to him, to any one man, ever again. Now we all belong to one another. We are the pack. We are one."

What am I supposed to make of this borderline-patricidal story,

Necra? Stanton wanted to ask. *Is your pack brainwashing my fake son to slit my throat and feed me to his pet Deinonychus?*

Instead, he said, "I appreciate you telling me that story. I do understand how you could choose this life, and you've obviously done a lot for your pack."

She sneered. Her pterosaur seemed to mimic her cold gaze. "You hide your calculating nature behind empty compliments, Ambassador."

"What have I done in all my days here except follow directions and answer all your questions?"

"You have bided your time. You have collected knowledge on us. You are plotting and scheming. I see behind your eyes."

Stanton maintained a stony expression. "I *am* plotting. Searching for leverage to negotiate. It's in my nature. I am happy to admit that. But I want you, the Alpha, the pack, everyone to understand that I no longer negotiate for Triassica." Then he allowed another pang of emotion to sink into his words, and he was surprised to find that it was genuine. "I am only thinking of Caleb now."

"Noble," Necra said. "If true."

Stanton took a bite of his dinosaur jerky. He gazed at the crystal blue sky and fluffy clouds, like spools of cotton. "Thank you for taking me up here," he said.

"My pleasure." She grinned. "Yah!" She whipped her arm, fingers spread in Stanton's direction. Immediately, the *Pteranodon* spread his wings and rushed forward, beak snapping.

Stanton tossed the jerky and pulled his arms over his face. The pterosaur pecked toward him. Hot air pressed around him as huge leathery wings flapped on either side. He shielded his eyes and tried to move left or right, but the flying behemoth kept snapping and lurching in whichever direction he headed. The clawed talons of its stubby legs scraped up dust as he flapped closer.

Stanton backed away. The finger-claws of the animal's wings grazed one shoulder and tore his jacket.

Necra screeched, whooped, and hollered. She cackled as the pterosaur pressed closer. Stanton neared the ledge. He glanced back and noticed it was only a meter to the charcoal ridge—and the long, horrible drop to where he would splatter amid hungry *Deinonychuses*.

"Necra!" he screamed. "Call it off! What are you doing?"

Necra laughed harder.

The *Pteranodon* poked his sharp face in the crook of Stanton's elbow and pushed him backward. He made a controlled drop and clawed at the ground as his feet and legs slid down the steep ledge.

Stanton screamed as the *Pteranodon* pecked at his hands, the only things keeping him from sliding all the way down.

At last, Necra rushed between them. She whispered soothing nonsense words, placed her hands on the sides of the pterosaur's face, and then fed him another rodent.

Stanton held on for dear life as the gray flyer guzzled his snack. Necra took a full ten seconds to shower her animal with praise and usher him away. The *Pteranodon* crawled back toward the center of the horn, and Necra's wild eyes gleamed down at Stanton.

For a long moment, he was certain that Necra wanted the pleasure of stomping his hands herself.

Eventually, she reached down and pulled him up with a Herculean grunt.

Then she pulled him close and whispered into his ear. "Any. Time. I want. Do not forget."

She stalked away toward her pet. Stanton collapsed onto his hands and knees. His whole body trembled. His heart convulsed.

Necra tied a note to the ankle of her *Pteranodon*, placed a kiss upon his crest, then shrieked and raised her arms to the sky. The pterosaur launched and soared upward, blotting out the sun.

16

Caleb stood centimeters from the steel cable fence that separated him from the snarling jaws and yellow eyes of a male *Carnotaurus*. The animal snorted; his tiny forearms twitched. He opened his mouth and a slimy, pale purple tongue slithered inside. Drool spilled between hooked yellow teeth.

The charcoal gray horns truly did resemble the enormous plateaus the raiders called home. The dinosaur's pen stretched a ninety-degree perimeter against the natural rock wall of the eastern horn. Midday sun sheened along the red-pebbled scales and armored plates of the *Carnotaurus*'s back.

Caleb scowled. "Bull-heads sure are ugly."

The dinosaur's nostrils flared against his smooshed, toothy snout.

"So are humans." Ajax towered behind Caleb. "Maybe that makes us compatible."

Caleb hadn't thought this far ahead about his raider training, that he'd be getting a crash course in herding big carnivores. He hardly believed he'd finally bonded with 44, but there was something plausible about that. A *Deinonychus*, though deadly, was smart, cunning. There was something human about that.

The bull-heads, with their stubby snouts and comically diminished forearms, seemed monsters through and through. Caleb glanced back at 44, wrestling a tumbleweed. He had tossed a stick for her to fetch almost five minutes ago, but before she reached it, she got distracted by a beetle.

Even if 44 couldn't always follow directions yet, she had all the charm and energy of a toddler. Caleb couldn't imagine even a hatchling *Carnotaurus* passing for cute. But he had to admit, 44 was winning him over.

"A *Carnotaurus* isn't a *Deinonychus*, so forget everything you've learned about 44 when dealing with them." Ajax tapped the metal shock prod strapped to his leg. "They need to be shocked into line. They need to be directed. *Deinonychus* are surgical. When you've got a rapport, you can use a slasher in battle like a scalpel. A *Carnotaurus* is more like a bomb. Set 'em loose and get the heck out of the way."

Caleb raised an eyebrow at Ajax. "I know how to get out of their way."

Ajax's expression grew stony, and he broke eye contact. "Of course you do."

Currently, four huge bull-heads occupied the raiders' spacious eastern pen. One raider climbed a ten-meter scaffolding on the north side of the enclosure and gave a long whistle. The devil-horned carnivores turned their round, toothy faces in unison and lumbered toward the north wall.

The raider kicked a barrel on its side. A disgusting waterfall of bloody slurry splattered into a long trough.

Caleb winced. "How do they live on that?"

"It's just day to day food," Ajax explained. "Like 44, sometimes they get a treat. They're encouraged to hunt when we take them out for exercise or…" He trailed off.

Caleb's face flushed with anger. "Or when you sic them on people."

Ajax cleared his throat. He wiped his brow. For the first time, Caleb's trainer seemed uncomfortable. "Carnotaurs are deadly. They don't always listen," he said. "Sometimes they might even go for one of us if we're not careful."

"That's why you killed the one in the cave," Caleb said. "How come it was even down there?"

"We study them. Breed them. They need medical care sometimes."

Caleb knew that Stanton was working in Necra's medical lab, but it occurred to him for the first time what a huge, delicate operation the raiders had going. The underground tunnels were complex, and between him and Stanton, they may have only seen half of what was down there.

By now, Caleb had gotten a good look at the exterior of the horns. There was a structure built against the east horn, but Ajax had explained it was a vehicle maintenance garage. "Do you have a hatchery?" he asked.

"A small one," Ajax said. "Many of our animals are reared in the west camp."

"That's where you train kids."

Ajax nodded. "I spent a lot of time out west. It's why the Alpha put me in charge of your training."

"So am I going in there?" Caleb asked. "Does 44 get a bull-head for a brother?" At the sound of her name, 44 came trouncing back toward them.

"44 is definitely not going in there," Ajax said. "They'd chomp her up. When she's grown more, they'll probably give her space."

44 skittered up, claws scraping dust. Her jaws were empty. "No!" Caleb said. He grabbed a new stick off the ground. He pointed emphatically at it. "Fetch, 44! Go get this and bring it back to me."

He hurled the stick into the distance. 44 darted after it, but within moments she was sniffing and digging under a rock, far from where the stick had landed. Caleb sighed.

"She'll learn. Don't worry. You think you're ready to go in there? A *Carnotaurus* isn't the same as a dryptosaur. Tougher skin. They're like tanks."

Caleb crossed his arms. "I know where the soft spots are."

"So do they." Ajax chuckled. "Keep taking risks, kid, you'll get yourself killed. I'll have a heck of a time explaining that to your dad."

Caleb grinned. "Tough talk, coming from a guy who's afraid of bugs."

Ajax jabbed Caleb's sternum with his finger. "Not a word of that to anyone!"

Armored *Carnotaurus* tails swayed above the trough; bloody snouts slurped at the slurry. V-shaped devil crests dipped up and down. Caleb let out a low whistle. "They sure are ugly."

"You were almost in that trough, you know," came a cold,

hardened voice.

Caleb glanced up. The Alpha's stern face contrasted his toothy tattooed grin. Caleb's mind flashed back to his first day under the horns. The Alpha clutching his once shaggy blond hair, exposing his neck to Necra's *Deinonychus*.

If you betray us, The Alpha had said, *his name will be Slurry. Do you understand the terms of this negotiation now, Ambassador Stanton?*

"Think about that next time you call them ugly." The Alpha's human smile spread. "Seconds away, you were, from being slurped up and shat out. Kinda funny, isn't it?"

Caleb gave a slow, uncertain nod.

Ajax cleared his throat. "Something you need?"

"Just doing rounds." The Alpha rubbed his chin and observed the feeding carnivores. "How is 44 working out for you, Caleb?"

"She's great," Caleb said. "We're bonding."

"Is that true, Ajax?"

Ajax nodded. "44's a runt, but she's a scrapper. Kinda like the kid here."

The Alpha beamed. He clapped Caleb's shoulder so hard it nearly sent him crashing against the cables of the carnivore pen. "You're getting a reputation."

Caleb shrugged. He locked eyes with the Alpha.

"In fact, I am beyond impressed with everything I've heard so far. You stuck a dryptosaur. You saved Ajax's life."

"We saved each other," Caleb said, quickly.

The Alpha clenched Caleb's shoulder. "That's right."

Caleb fought the urge to shove the Alpha's hand away.

"Are you starting to feel like part of the pack?" The Alpha pinched the fingers of his other hand apart. "Maybe just... a little?"

How should I answer this? Caleb wondered. "So long as my dad is safe," he said, "I'm one of you."

The Alpha crouched. He looked Caleb up and down. Then he tapped the metal claw strapped to Caleb's thigh. "What's this?" He smiled at Ajax.

"Caleb earned it." Ajax folded his arms. "He's allowed to have it on him, so long as I'm present."

The Alpha stood tall and whistled. "I think we've got ourselves a prodigy. I never imagined Stanton's kid would be an all-star." He shook his head. "You must have had some mom!" Then he howled with laughter.

Caleb clenched his fists. His face burned. "Don't talk about my mom."

The Alpha scowled.

"You're speaking out of turn, Caleb." Ajax placed a hand on Caleb's shoulder. "You don't tell the Alpha what to do."

"That's right. I'll always be in charge." The inked horns on the Alpha's brow narrowed. "Unless you kill me."

Caleb gritted his teeth.

"It really is a curiosity," the Alpha said. "You being such a survivor."

"Caleb's mother died in childbirth," Ajax explained. "His uncle trained him in survival, when he was younger, while Stanton worked."

Caleb glanced back and forth between Ajax and the Alpha. He

had mentioned an "uncle" only one time. There was no story about training. Caleb quickly muttered, "My dad... he's tougher than he seems."

"He's sly, and he's kind of proud of it." The Alpha folded his hands behind his back and paced a semi-circle around them. "I like your dad, kid. I do."

"Caleb is more than a compound brat," Ajax said. "He's traveled with his dad and his uncle. He's spent as much time in the wild as behind Triassica's walls."

Caleb nodded. *I never said that. Not exactly. Is Ajax assuming? Or covering for me?*

The Alpha nodded. "Either way, he's an impressive young man."

What is this all about? Caleb wondered. *Am I being cross-examined? Did something happen to Stanton?*

"You're good with that claw, huh?" The Alpha asked. The distant chuffing of carnivores and slurry continued. *Pteranodons* screeched atop the western horn.

"I got lucky," Caleb said. "That's all." Then against his better judgement, he added, "I'm better with an ax."

The Alpha laughed. "I know. A pickax! That's what you drove through our *Deinonychus*. Swung it like a natural born miner."

Caleb froze.

The Alpha unbuckled the holster at his side and slid out his own barbed, three-pronged wrist claw. He began to strap it to his right hand. "Tell you what, Caleb. I'd love to see what you've got."

Caleb's stomach sank. He could feel the color draining from his face.

"We haven't sparred with claws yet," Ajax explained. "He's not ready for—"

"Are *you* speaking out of turn now, Ajax?" The Alpha's eyes blazed. "Telling your Alpha what to do?"

Ajax paused. "I'm reporting Caleb's progress. I want my Alpha to be informed."

"Good save," The Alpha whispered. "I prefer a more hands on approach in understanding the skillsets at my disposal." He secured the strap around his wrist and pointed his claw at Caleb. "Put yours on."

Caleb's hands trembled as he unsheathed and strapped the claw to his wrist.

"Come at me, Caleb." The Alpha nodded. Sun gleamed on the barbs of his claws. "With everything you've got."

Caleb shook his head. He glanced back at Ajax, whose blazing red beard stood in stark contrast to the pallid skin around his eyes. He faced the double carnivore grin of the Alpha.

"Don't be shy, compound brat," The Alpha crooned. "I just want to see what you've got."

Dozens of voices competed in Caleb's mind.

There was Ambassador Stanton begging him to keep his head down, to not make any move before they were ready.

There was Ajax, warning him to be careful. To know his place in the pack.

And then there was his own voice, crying out for this man—this *murderer's*—blood.

"Come on, Caleb," the Alpha whispered. "Pretend I'm a

dryptosaur."

This was obviously a test, but whether Caleb failed or passed, he could end up dead.

The Alpha's muscles tensed, tightening the dinosaur skeleton of his tattoos. The blades of his claw gleamed.

"If I kill you," Caleb whispered. "Then I become the Alpha."

"That's a mighty big if, Caleb," Ajax whispered.

The Alpha only raised his eyebrows invitingly.

"If I'm the Alpha…" Caleb said.

"Then you and your pop are basically free." The Alpha nodded. "That's what you want, right?"

Pteranodons cried. Bull-heads slurped. The Alpha's bald head glistened.

Caleb took a deep controlled breath, and he slipped into a fighting stance.

"Caleb…" Ajax warned.

Across the clearing, 44 perked up and chirped in alarm. Her feathers bristled, and she scampered in their direction.

"You make the first move, Caleb." The Alpha's voice dipped into an odd soothing tone. "I'm ready when you are."

"Caleb, you don't have to," Ajax said.

"He's ordering me to." Caleb tightened his grip on his claw.

44 came snapping between Caleb and the Alpha. She twisted around and snorted at the hulking man with the claw.

"44 get back," Caleb said. "Don't hurt her."

The Alpha only chuckled. "Don't be silly." He stepped forward and got down on one knee. Then he stroked 44's feathery neck with his left hand. "She's one of *mine*." He whispered sweet sounds, then slapped the animal's shoulder.

44 squawked and skittered behind Caleb. She twisted back around and shrank away from the Alpha in submission.

Heat rose into Caleb's cheeks. *She's not yours*, he thought. *I'm not yours. None of this is yours.* He screamed and rushed forward, claw reared back, ready to stab.

In an instant, the Alpha sidestepped and grabbed Caleb by his vest. He swung him through the air and slammed him onto his back. Caleb's head hit the dusty ground and stars splattered his vision. The Alpha pressed Caleb's clawed hand against his ribcage then stuck the barbed tips of his claws at Caleb's neck.

"Just what I thought," the Alpha said. "Sloppy. Not sure why you gave this kid a claw, Ajax." He leaned in close. His breath smelled like dinosaur jerky. "But I like you, Caleb. I truly do."

The Alpha released his wrist and stood.

Caleb trembled; tears streamed down his cheeks.

Ajax's face burned crimson. 44 chirped in alarm between the two hulking men. "Was that necessary?" Ajax snarled.

"You've been questioning me a lot lately," the Alpha said to him. "If you're going to give that kid a claw, make sure you train him how to use it."

The Alpha marched along the perimeter of the fence. A *Carnotaurus* strode up alongside him and roared for his attention.

Caleb struggled to his knees. He fought back tears. And then the voice of Ambassador Stanton crept back into his mind. *Use this*, Stanton urged. *You're upset, fine, be upset. Ajax is upset too. Use that.*

Ajax helped him to his feet. "Relax, kid," he said. "You're okay."

Caleb shoved Ajax's hands away. "I'm fine," his voice broke. He wiped tears on his wrists, and absentmindedly nicked his cheek with the top of his claw. He groaned with frustration.

"Take that off. Put it away," Ajax started to unstrap the claw.

Caleb twisted away. "I said I'm fine!" Blood from his cheek dripped onto the dusty ground. 44 trotted up to him and nuzzled his stomach. He cradled her head in his arm.

Ajax stood at a loss for words.

Caleb sniffled, then broke the silence. "You said the Alpha isn't the toughest. He's just the toughest guy who wanted the job."

Ajax nodded.

"You never answered my question: Why don't *you* want the job?"

17

"Ajax said *what?*" Stanton had listened with interest to Caleb's recounting of the day's events, but he wanted to be clear about this last part. "Were those his *exact* words?"

"Verbatim." Caleb sat on the edge of his cot and scratched 44's fiery neck. "He said, 'Maybe I do.'"

Stanton rubbed his chin, "As in maybe he wants to be the Alpha."

Caleb whispered. "He would let us go, I'm sure of it."

"We've seen too much," Stanton said. "Ajax might be less crazy than the Alpha. He might even genuinely like you, Caleb, but there's no way he'll let us go."

"He's not like the rest of them," Caleb insisted. "He's never been on raids. He was a trainer. He worked with kids."

Stanton sighed. "Maybe. But, Caleb, don't forget, we only know what they tell us."

"He covered for me," Caleb said. "It seemed like the Alpha suspected that you and I weren't related, and Ajax started talking about my uncle, trying to explain where I learned to hunt dinosaurs."

"And maybe Ajax did that so he and the Alpha could see if you'd correct him," Stanton said.

Caleb fell silent.

"I hope that's not the case, but listen, if you can find out how soon Ajax plans to challenge the Alpha—if it's even true—that might be a good night for us to slip away, while everyone's distracted by the potential shift in power."

"He's going to do it." Caleb smiled. "And when he does, all we'll have to do is work with him. He'll fix all of this."

"You're putting a lot of faith in Ajax," Stanton said.

"Fine." Caleb shrugged and laid back. 44 rested her head on his chest. "What about you? What happened today?"

"Necra took me to the top of the western horn. There's an elevator that runs from the cave system to the top. Solar panels up there, good view of the surrounding area." Stanton gave an exhausted sigh. "God, it felt good to be outside. You're lucky you've been out as much as you have."

"Yeah, lucky me," Caleb muttered.

"Necra has a system with the *Pteranodons*. She gets messages from the raiders' western camp. She's as good with the pterosaurs as she is with the slashers. It's eerie."

"What else happened?" Caleb asked. The lights cut out, plunging them into their usual nine p.m. shadows.

Stanton hesitated. "Not much else. Busy work in the lab. I got a glimpse of carnivore pens in the cave system on the way to and from the elevator. There may be stimulants held near that area."

"That's it, huh?"

"Yeah," he said. "That's it. We should sleep. Who knows what curveballs they'll throw us tomorrow." Guilt sank into Stanton's stomach. He should have told Caleb about the attack, that he'd nearly slipped off the edge when Necra unleashed her pet.

Was it that he didn't want to rattle Caleb? Didn't want him to be any more scared than he was? No, that wasn't it. It was pride, and he knew it. Stanton was ashamed that Caleb could stick a dryptosaur at thirteen, and he himself couldn't defend against the frantic wings of a single *Pteranodon*.

Stanton was no Ajax. No wonder the kid had shifted his hopes to his trainer.

Stanton's mind drifted back to his own childhood. Caleb's false backstory was starting to mirror the true upbringing of Niles Stanton. It was baby Niles who had killed his mother in childbirth, not Caleb. It was Niles who had been raised by survivalists—not his uncle, but his father and two older brothers.

Niles was no compound brat; but he would have loved to have grown up in Triassica. Most assuredly, his father would have preferred Caleb as a son.

Joe used to say that Niles had been born into tragedy. Niles's brothers and father spoke of their mother with reverence normally reserved for deities. And while his family had loved and cared for him growing up, Niles carried the chip on his shoulder that his mother—tough as a T. rex, gentle as a *Maiasaura*—had left the world all for Niles's sake.

Young Niles had a great propensity for words, but little aptitude for wrestling and skinning *Dimetrodons* in the putrid southern swamps where his father camped for half the year.

The Stanton clan were swamp rats. And Niles, as Joe often put it, had risen "above all that" when his charisma unlocked the compound gates.

Niles's father Roger Stanton had grown up in a farming town in the midlands. The town decayed into poverty with the rise of the three compounds: Triassica, Jurassica, and Cretacia. Many of Roger's family and neighbors were among the first to sign up for the Cretacia waiting list.

But the promise of a safe, organized society had bored teenage Roger to tears. He hooked up with the spitfire preacher's daughter Eileen Lash; they sold their earthly possessions and invested in the construction of an all-terrain trailer. Nine months after they hit the road, they brought Niles's oldest brother Clint into the fold.

Clint was swiftly followed by Chester, what the Stantons' very distant ancestors apparently referred to as "Irish twins." For a time, the Stanton family lived happily ever after as trappers and hunters. They exterminated big carnivores nesting too close to the budding compound of Cretacia. They vended meat to local butchers and made tools and weapons from dinosaur claws, horns, and bones.

Eileen Stanton could "sew a burlap sack into a three-piece suit," as Roger once explained to his motherless thirdborn. It was a skill she failed to pass on to her first two sons, but Niles wore all the hand-me-downs: durable cargo pants, shirts, vests, jackets, and caps for chill nights.

The Stantons were the posterchild family for what many southern frontier folk called "Living Free." They suffered no compound regulations or oversight. They were multi-skilled survivors turning profits and following the action, a New Pangea fairytale come true.

Until Niles.

Without Eileen—and the added burden of a baby—Roger struggled to procure and produce the same goods the family had once yielded. All the profits seemed to go into keeping their mobile home running.

Niles's brothers were nine and ten years older than him. Clint was a tough guy and interrogator. When brokenhearted Dad sank into a jar of moonshine, the older Clint would order Chester around and assume the position of head of the family. It fell upon Chester by default to care for Niles, and while he did a good enough job, his brother's heart was never in the role of parent.

Niles knew he was a burden from a very young age. In fact, his yearning for acceptance by his father and brothers gave way to his passion for negotiation. In time, that passion *did* serve his family.

By the age of nine, it was Niles—not Roger, Clint, or Chester—who brokered deals with compound representatives. Even as a small boy, Niles observed and understood the nuances of supply and demand. He recommended to his father what to hunt, when, and why. He would suggest that they withhold stock and present it in times of desperation. "People pay more for blankets when they're cold, Dad," he'd say.

On one summer day, the Stantons drove their goods into the heart of Cretacia for a trade festival. Niles fell in love with the towering marble structures, fountains, fashionable clothes, and warm urban customers. He noted the women flocking to the theater—a concept as foreign to him as sky to a fish. They wore bright blue, red, and green feathers over their perfectly styled hair.

"*Archaeopteryx* hats!" he had shouted in epiphany as they left the glistening metropolis behind them that night. "The women, Dad! Their hats are designed with *Archaeopteryx* feathers."

His dad had given him a cock-eyed glare of disapproval at that. "Why the hell do you care about some froofy ladies' hats?"

Niles sighed with exasperation. "Because they're easy to catch, right? They'll *pay* for them." Truthfully, Niles *had* been smitten with the idea of dressing up to go someplace cultured—the places he only visited in books he stashed under his bunk.

But the glamor of the theater was beside the point. He twisted his father's arm in the weeks between their next opportunity to sell in Cretacia. His brothers relentlessly teased him.

"Niles just wants to wear ladies' hats."

"Don't get upset, you little *Archaeopteryx* princess."

"Let's make him a nice training bra out of *Dimorphodon* wings!"

By the time Niles was ten, these insults rolled off his back, of course, and his father, indifferent to his sons' teasing, always had an inkling when Niles was onto something.

Roger set his boys to work one day, trapping as many *Archaeopteryxes* as they could find. When they returned to market, they made a killing from smitten, upper-crust Cretacians. The compounds were all about equity, Niles quickly learned, but luxury was somehow exempt from that—particularly with Cretacians— and Roger too was shocked to learn that the truly valuable goods they brokered—basic elements of survival—yielded less money than the froofy hat-birds.

"Thank God, your momma left me with one smart one," his father had said, clapping Niles affectionately on the shoulder that day. But Roger Stanton never failed to undermine praise for his third son. "You don't have your brothers' brawn, but those brains count for something," he added.

Lying in the darkness of the raiders' stronghold, Niles could almost smell the swamp gas. He could picture that campsite—their mobile home parked on some inlet, clotheslines strung between trees. They would set up huge severed *Dimetrodon* sails with bright green and yellow "eye" patterns on the webs between the spines. The dried sails flanked all sides of the camp like an alien garden.

The sight of the sails warded off small predators like *Coelophysis*. Incandescent lanterns hung from tree branches and steel rods. Chemical incense repelled mosquitos.

Clint and Chester used to play horseshoes in the afternoons. They'd never even seen a picture of a horse, but they picked up the rules and inherited the metal Us from an ancient man who lived on the edge of the desert. Clinks and clanks echoed in Niles's memory, along with his brothers' snarky, but loving, insults. He'd sit there and scour his body for leeches that he'd burn off using a hot stick that he'd held to a torch. The boys would pass the evening whittling wood and bone, carving tools and knick-knacks that sometimes sold in western towns.

And Roger would drink.

Niles never dared tell his father how much of their profits went toward moonshine. He knew that part of getting along with his dad was allowing him to numb his regrets.

Once when Niles was twelve, his brothers retired early, exhausted from a day of wrangling, gutting, and packing *Dimetrodon* meat in salty barrels. Niles sat under twinkling stars. He tied snares for the next day's work and listened to the symphonic chitters and moans of the primordial swamp.

His glassy-eyed father placed a hand on his shoulder. "Niles, son, I want you to know something." His voice broke. "I'm not mad that you're queer. These things happen. It's normal. The more boys you have…" He shrugged. "One turns out that way. It's God's way of keeping the population of men under control, maybe."

Niles had been stunned speechless. He himself hadn't even articulated his sexuality in his own mind yet. He understood, of course, that his thoughts and impulses and glances leaned that way, but a life of hunting and evading monsters hadn't afforded him the luxury to worry about it.

His father slurped from his mason jar. Fireflies gave cool green flashes all around them. "Perfectly okay, son. No, that doesn't bother me. To lose your mother to gain a son. That's a blessing, and I'm not upset that you're that way."

And for a moment, tears of joy welled in Niles's eyes, as if a problem had been perfectly solved before it had ever begun.

Then his father—like always—had to ruin it. "I just wish you weren't weak."

Niles's stomach sank like a stone, and tears did flow, but not joyful ones.

"A queer son who can handle himself," Roger Stanton slurred.

"I'd be proud enough of that."

That night, lying in the rusty trailer that reeked of his brothers' body odor, Niles began to yearn for the compound. To walk a clean street. Live with a roof over his head. To be the man who negotiated with swamp people, not the swamp boy begging to be heard and understood.

Sooner than he had imagined, young Niles would have his wish, at great cost.

The *click-clack* of the door latch interrupted Stanton's reverie. A sliver of firelight shone as the door to their cell creaked open. 44 perked up; her eyes glowed. Caleb gave a heavy breath, but did not stir.

Niles sat up. The Alpha loomed in the doorway, calloused knuckles clutching the handle of his lantern, skeletal tattoos swaying with shadows.

"Leave your son," the Alpha commanded. "And follow me."

18

Stanton followed the Alpha through dark, silent caverns. They passed a lone raider scrubbing moss and lichen off the cave wall. Night sentries passed and nodded in respect at the Alpha as they crossed the main cavern. They proceeded into the winding passage toward the *Carnotaurus* holding pens and the elevator.

Are we going up again? Stanton wondered. *Am I pterosaur food after all?*

But they passed the elevator shaft and descended a crooked metal staircase. White lights shone at the end of a long corridor. Pained moans reverberated. A woman whispered in soothing, patronizing tones. *Necra.*

"I'm sure you expected this," the Alpha said.

"Another lab?" Stanton asked. "I had assumed."

"The real lab," The Alpha said. "It's time for you to understand."

They entered a semi-circular opening in the cave system. The ceilings and walls had been ground smooth. Metal cabinets, shelves and tables lined the walls, along with sophisticated equipment—beakers, burners, chemical drips. *Necra learned a lot from her father's books,* Stanton thought.

In the center of the room, Necra loomed over a metal table,

where a large, pallid man lay, his barrel chest and belly exposed. She cradled one large palm in her hand and wiped sweat off his tattooed brow. The man's red beard was matted against his chest. His lip quivered with misery.

It was Ajax.

"Rest," Necra whispered. "Rest."

Ajax vainly attempted words. Glassy eyes turned in his sockets. His soaked cargo pants had been rolled up to his knees, and cobalt veins shone against paper-white ankles. The air reeked of sweat and urine.

Stanton recoiled, but the Alpha marched up to Ajax and gave a slow, somber shake of his head.

"What happened?" Stanton whispered.

"Bull-Fever," the Alpha said.

Ajax's arms convulsed; his fingers twisted into claws. Red foam dribbled from his lips.

Stanton recalled little more than a week ago, Ajax gutting the feral *Carnotaurus* in the main hub of the cave system. How the blood had splattered over him. The Alpha had looked Ajax up and down and said, *You'd better wash up.*

"I don't sss…" Ajax hissed for a word that couldn't quite come, then squeezed his feverish eyes.

"Don't bother," Necra whispered. "Just rest."

The Alpha placed a hand on Ajax's shoulder. "It's a true shame," he said, looking down at Ajax. "If anyone here—other than myself, of course—was fit to be Alpha, it would have been him."

Stanton felt the color drain from his face. With nothing but a sack of cotton swabs under his head, Ajax was laid up like a corpse on the autopsy table. The Alpha was speaking of him like he had already died.

Tears streamed down Ajax's cheeks.

Did the Alpha know? Stanton wondered. *Did he expect Ajax to challenge?*

"Why did you bring me here?" Stanton asked.

"To show you this." The Alpha gestured over Ajax's quivering form. "This, Ambassador Stanton, is what you will bring back to Triassica."

Nausea gripped Stanton's stomach. He leaned forward and gagged. Necra placed a bucket in front of him. He fell to his knees and puked into it.

"This is a sterile environment, Stanton," she said. "Compose yourself."

"It's all right, Necra." The Alpha caressed Ajax's bald head. "Ambassador Stanton's revulsion to disease is natural. I myself had never imagined harnessing a virus the way we might harness a carnivore, but Necra proved to me that it can be done."

The Alpha circled Ajax. His tattooed hand curled around one of three gray cannisters. Stanton composed himself. He made uneasy eye contact with Ajax as he approached the cannisters, each labeled in Necra's scrawling script with a series of letters and numbers— different strains? Different potencies?

"We've known about the virus for a long time, but it appeared to only be carried by *Carnotaurus*. Necra observed that when an infected carnotaur went into the slurry, the *Deinonychus* that ate it got sick. We acquired more sophisticated instruments for collecting samples and set up this lab here.

"Within time, Necra perfected a process for synthesizing and replicating a pure strain. A perfect weapon to slip through impenetrable walls, past sophisticated weapons."

The Alpha took Stanton's hand and placed it on one of the cannisters. He placed his own calloused, ink-covered fingers over Stanton's. "When you return to Triassica, you will smuggle Necra's virus in. You will take it to the central water filtration facility, and you will distribute it."

Stanton's guts turned again, but he managed to keep it down. For a moment, he forgot all about Caleb, all about playing the long game of wait and see. "How could I ever do that?" he whispered.

"Because once every man, woman, and child in Triassica are dead behind their impenetrable walls, only then will I return your son to you."

The Alpha turned his attention back to the dying man on the table. "In spirit, Ajax will march those walls with us. In the pack, he lives on."

Ajax writhed and cried out.

The Alpha gripped Stanton's shoulders. "I understand that you are not prepared to do this today. I understand that it will take time to acclimate you to this plan. That you must give no outward sign of suspicion in delivering this task. We will work on that together."

Stanton nodded. Tears spilled down his cheeks.

"I believe in you, Ambassador Stanton," the Alpha said. "I believe you when you tell me that we must have trust. We will have trust. Is that understood?"

He nodded again.

"Say 'Yes.' Out loud." The Alpha's fingers dug into his skin.

"Yes," Stanton's voice came out hollow and distant. "For Caleb… I'll do it."

"Tomorrow at dinner, you will tell me the cover story that you will use when you reappear in Triassica alive. You were taken by us. There was a harrowing escape. Your son tragically did not make it. Talk me through that. Come up with the details. Then we'll review the logistics of your reentry and a timeline for infection."

Necra took the canisters and, one by one, carried them to a gray refrigerator case. She slipped them in one at a time, then placed a keycode operated padlock on the lid. "I need to draw blood," she said. "I want to run more tests."

"Can it wait?" The Alpha said.

"Science does not wait." She approached and addressed the Alpha over Ajax's shivering body. "And it is also important that you understand this process. Should I ever meet an unfortunate accident." The corners of her lips hooked up at that.

Ajax rasped.

"All right, then." The Alpha clapped Stanton's shoulder. "Stay with Ajax. I wouldn't want him to die alone. We'll be back shortly."

Necra gathered a syringe and medical bag and led the Alpha down the winding hallway. As their boots clanked up the crooked staircase, something snatched Stanton's wrist.

"Stanton!" Ajax's voice scraped.

Stanton twisted around to find Ajax's face red as a cherry, his whole body shaking. "I'm not as gone… as they think… not yet… but will be."

"I'm sorry."

The raider's glassy eyes widened; tears slipped into the rank tangles of his beard. "Protect. That. Boy!"

"I will," Stanton whispered.

"Get him out of here!"

"Give me something I can use!"

"Seven, eight, four, six," Ajax chanted. "Seven, eight, four, six. Seven, eight, four, six… They change the sequence sometimes… not as often as they should."

Stanton nodded. The weapons cases, the vehicle keys. If he was lucky, maybe even Necra's fridge.

"Seven, eight, four, six," Stanton said. "Seven, eight, four, six."

"Yes…" Ajax unleashed a volley of coughs. Bloody froth bubbled under his tongue. He struggled to speak.

Stanton covered his mouth with his shirt.

"Has to be ingested," Ajax finally managed to say. "Or blood to blood. You won't catch it from me…"

Stanton pulled his shirt down and moved closer.

"Listen." Ajax coughed again. "They'll tell everyone it was… when I gutted the rogue bull… *They* did it. Necra… sat with me at dinner… came over me in a matter of hours… If I had the strength… I'd…" Another series of horrible coughs.

"You'd kill them where they stand. Damnit, Ajax, why did you wait? Why did you ever let him run things in the first place?"

More tears leaked down Ajax's weathered face. "Because I'm…

bad as them… We're all monsters."

Stanton squeezed the dying man's palm. "Caleb doesn't think of you that way."

"Stanton," Ajax wheezed. "If you're that kid's dad, then my mom was a bloody spinosaur." He coughed. "Don't know… if you love that kid or not… but I like the hell out of him."

Stanton nodded. "I do too. You covered for us today. Does the Alpha suspect?"

"Don't know." Ajax gagged and blood trickled into his beard. "Always thought you people were privileged pricks… but… when I looked in Caleb's eyes. I saw ghosts… I thought maybe… maybe I put them there."

"Seven, eight, four, six," Stanton chanted under his breath. "Seven, eight, four, six."

"Told Caleb…" Ajax's voice broke. His grip tightened. "I never raided Columbia… I lied. Just wanted him to relax."

Stanton shook his head. "Did you kill his parents?"

"No way of knowing," Ajax confessed. "They would have meant nothing to me. If I had never met him… don't think I would have cared."

"Seven, eight, four, six," Stanton whispered. "What else, Ajax? What else can you tell us?"

"Canteen," Ajax said. "In my pocket."

"You want water?"

"No…" his eyes rolled back. "Take it… Find a way to… give Necra… medicine…"

"Ajax!" Stanton whispered.

The raider's head rolled to one side. He struggled. His eyes fluttered.

"Ajax!"

Foam settled on his lips.

Stanton felt Ajax's weakening pulse. The rectangular shape of the canteen showed in his cargo pocket. "Seven, eight, four, six," he whispered. He glanced at the padlock on the fridge, then frantically unbuttoned the pocket and removed the canteen. He unscrewed the top, rushed to the wash basin at the end of the room, and dumped the contents.

Necra's medicine! He hurried to the padlock on the refrigerator and keyed in the code: *Seven, eight, four, six.* He pulled the padlock. Nothing.

Seven, four, six, eight. Nothing.

"Come on!" *Seven, six, eight, four.* Nothing.

He continued to mix up the numbers to no avail, suddenly aware that he'd probably begun repeating combinations. What was the original order? *Seven, eight, four, six.* He keyed it in backward. *Six, four, eight, seven. Pop!*

Stanton yanked off the padlock and set it aside. He listened closely: no returning steps down the metal staircase. He opened the fridge. Cool steam washed out. He pulled out a gray cannister and carried it to the sink. He carefully positioned Ajax's canteen in the bottom of the sink, twisted the top off the cannister, and—slowly, steadily—poured a thin stream of clear liquid into the narrow mouth of the canteen.

He grabbed a towel off a drying rack and used it to carefully close and wipe the edges of the canteen.

He filled the cannister back to the top with water from the pipe, until it weighed the same as before, then screwed it shut.

Ajax's breaths heaved a terrible death rattle.

Stanton wiped the canteen and canister and returned the towel to its rack. Then he rushed to the refrigerator and returned the canister beside the other two. He twisted it until Necra's label faced the same direction as the others. Just as he was about to close the door, he noticed rows of vials with bright yellow tape, clearly labeled.

The carnivore stimulants.

Not enough time, he thought to himself. He shut the door and clipped the padlock back into place.

Stanton slipped the canteen in his pocket but cringed at the bulky shape it made against his thigh. *They'll see that.* He scoured the lab.

Ajax's breaths trembled.

Stanton flipped open cabinets until he found a roll of medical tape. He removed his vest, yanked his shirt up and tucked it under his chin, then he pulled a long strap of white tape and stuck it to his abdomen. He held the canteen behind him with one hand and carefully wound the roll of tape back until it hugged the toxic canteen against the small of his back.

The tape complained with a loud sticky sound as he yanked and wound strap after strap. He pulled it as tight against his body as possible, until he'd fastened the entire canteen, top to bottom against his back.

Ajax's rattles grew further apart.

The steady *clank-clank* of boots on stairs echoed. Stanton yanked his shirt down and put his vest back on, praying it was loose-fitting enough that nobody would notice, that the tape would not snap when he tried to move.

He returned the tape to the cabinet, just as the Alpha and Necra reappeared.

"What are you doing?" Necra demanded.

Stanton steadied his breath. He continued to rummage through the cabinet. "Looking for painkillers," he said. "To alleviate Ajax's suffering."

"Close that cabinet," Necra ordered. "Ajax is a warrior. Pain is an old friend of his, come to bid him farewell."

Stanton slammed the cabinet and glared at Necra and the Alpha. "He was kind to my son," Stanton said. "It was the only thing I could think to do for him."

Silence filled the lab. Ajax's chest stopped moving. His breaths ceased.

"He is gone now," Necra said.

"Who will train my son now?"

The Alpha approached Ajax's still form. "Caleb's safety is a top priority, integral to our working relationship." He closed Ajax's glassy eyes and smiled his cruel double-smile. "I will hand select his next trainer. If you find that person unsatisfactory, then I will train him myself."

19

Midnight had approached by the time the Alpha escorted Stanton back to his room. Caleb and 44 waited, both awake. When the Alpha left them, Stanton broke the news.

Caleb broke out in sobs. He buried his face in 44's feathery shoulder. The animal crooned, and in a shockingly human gesture, placed a clawed hand on the boy's knee. "He was the only good one," Caleb repeated over and over.

Stanton decided to keep Ajax's confession to himself.

When Caleb calmed down, Stanton quietly shared the Alpha's plans. By one a.m., he felt confident the Alpha would not return unexpectedly.

He removed his shirt and carefully tore the medical tape from his body, yanking hair in painful strips. Caleb helped him remove the last few strands and secure the infectious canteen. "Be extremely careful."

Stanton slid under his cot and used the medical tape, which had lost much of its stick, but retained its strength, to tie the canteen between the bars of the bed frame. He used the faint glow of his watch to work in the dark.

"So far the raiders haven't searched the room for contraband."

He finished tying the last strap of tape, tucked it under the mattress, and slid back out with a grunt. "Let's hope they don't start now."

Caleb hunched in darkness. 44 licked his fingers between empathetic croons.

Stanton sat beside him. "I told you when this all started that my top priority was to get us—to get you—out alive," he said. "But that if I could get you revenge, I would. I don't have it all worked out yet, but I think you just might get it."

Caleb's voice came out raw and weary. "Why did he have to die?"

"It's New Pangea, kid." Stanton shook his head. "It's no picnic, and it never will be."

Caleb sighed.

"I was an orphan too," he said. "But my family wasn't murdered. I don't know how terrible that must feel, and... I'm sorry."

"It's not your fault," Caleb said. "You were there to help us. If we'd had walls..."

Stanton's stomach turned.

"How did your family die?" Caleb asked.

"My dad and my brothers were hunters and trappers," Stanton said. "I helped broker the deal, when I was your age, to pull jobs for the Council of Cretacia. The compounds were young then. They were always having problems with predators. My brothers could kill *Dimetrodons* in their sleep. Me, I hated it. I lost track of how many times I almost lost an arm as a kid. Eventually, my dad ordered me to stay out of the water.

"When you're that age, you think your dad and older brothers are invincible. I thought, if we could slay a *Baryonyx*, why not something bigger."

44 tucked her snout into Caleb's lap.

"What got them?" Caleb asked.

"The King himself," Stanton said. "T. rex. We only wounded her. Enraged her. We retreated to our trailer. Her mate emerged from the woods. They ripped the roof right off that old rust-bucket. My brother Clint pushed me into the closet. He covered me in blankets. I heard them screaming.

"I remember how, suddenly, it was so quiet. Then the ground quaked after the rexes lost interest and departed. And when I crawled out… that was it."

"They *were* murdered," Caleb said. "By carnivores. Same as my parents."

"No humans drugged up those rexes and weaponized them, Caleb. It's not the same. My family went looking for a fight. We got it. The compound rep Anthony Nash felt terrible. He petitioned to bring me into Cretacia and took me under his roof. I went to school for the first time in my life. I liked it there."

"How did you end up in Triassica?" Caleb asked.

Stanton blushed. "Nash was a good man, but he was upset when I fell in love with his son Joe."

"Joe Nash?" Caleb said. "From the Columbia Triumvirate?"

Stanton nodded. "Joe and I thought it would be easier on his family if we petitioned for roles in one of the other compounds. We did well in Triassica. Compound life rewards same-sex couples, so long as you have 'social value,' as they call it. They like that you're not going to reproduce. Population control."

"That's why Triassica founded Columbia in the first place," Caleb said. "Too many people. They needed space."

"That and the prospect of the mine," Stanton said.

"So how come you didn't come with Joe?" Caleb's innocent inflection hung in darkness for a long moment.

"He wanted kids." Stanton shrugged. "He wanted to adopt, to raise a child together, an orphan like I had been… like you. We were both climbing the ranks at Triassica, and he thought we had enough swing to petition it."

"You didn't want kids?"

"I wasn't sure. I knew we would be rocking the boat. They let us in originally because they were sure we *couldn't* reproduce. But Joe just… wanted to be a dad. I guess it's not that I didn't want that; I didn't think I'd be any good at it. And after so long of being with someone, when you have a big disconnect like that, Caleb… I don't need to go into all of this with you, but… Joe and I just kind of fell apart. He took the Columbia job for the same reason we left Cretacia. We each needed the distance to move forward."

"I don't understand that," Caleb said. "You love someone so much that you want them far away?"

"It is hard to understand," Stanton agreed. "I hope you don't ever go through it." He gave a weak laugh. "Actually, if you do, it means we'll have gotten through this."

44 gave a sleepy kick, her curved claw scraped the wall. Caleb roused her and her serrated mouth gave a gaping yawn. "We should sleep." The boy climbed onto his cot and 44 curled at the foot.

Stanton got into bed. "Caleb." Tears burned the corners of his eyes. "We need to trust each other."

"I know."

"I have to tell you something. I'm so sorry. But I was not there to give Columbia walls. I was there to deny support."

Stony silence.

"And I regret it. If I could do it over again, I would have fought harder for all of you. You did not deserve this."

Another long pause. "You would have left us all to die?"

"It's not like that…"

"What is it like then?"

Stanton struggled to explain the compound politics, the resource allocation, the net loss of the mining operation, the intentions versus the reality. All of it seemed to choke up in his mouth. It would come out sounding as absurd as telling Joe to leave because he loved him too much.

Caleb's voice cut through cold darkness. "You're as bad as the raiders if that's what you were doing. At least they ink themselves on the outside, so we know they're monsters."

20

Until the small hours of the morning, Caleb festered with grief—for his parents, for Ajax. Rage seethed under his skin. He despised the Alpha and his raiders for their culture of murder. He hated Triassica for displacing and endangering hundreds of people then refusing to help. How could Ambassador Stanton ever live with being a cog in their machine?

The soft touch of 44's feathers seemed the only anchor left in the world. He held her like a raft at sea. *She's the only one alive who hasn't betrayed me—a freakin' slasher!* He massaged the sleeping *Deinonychus*'s back.

What began as a weak laugh turned into a shocking pulse of guilt. *Am I any better, befriending her after I slaughtered her kind—animals that had nothing to do with my parents' deaths?*

Eventually sleep claimed him, but he had barely drifted off when the wrenching metal door jarred him back awake. His addled mind fully expected Ajax's mountainous form in the doorway.

Instead Necra leaned on the metal frame, her wiry arms crossed. "Get up!"

Caleb did not so much as glance in Ambassador Stanton's direction as they marched through the hub. Necra took Caleb and

44 as far as the short passageway to the arena. The woman spoke directly to Stanton. "Your spawn is to wait in the arena for his new instructor." She pointed down the hallway.

"Caleb—" Stanton started.

"I have ears!" Caleb marched toward the arena. He patted his thigh and 44 trotted after him.

As Caleb and 44 waited in the arena, he examined the cases of combat weapons: skewers, wrist claws, sabers, knives, saws, staffs, spears, and—of course—his father's tyrannosaur bone knife.

Caleb knew that tranqs and shock prods were in the cabinets near the panic gates at the top of the freight elevator. Like most valuables, the arena weapons were under coded padlock, but they now knew the four magic numbers: *Seven, eight, four, six.*

He yearned to try the combination and pull a weapon. He wanted to slash the throat of whoever was coming to train him. *To hell with Ambassador Stanton's plans. He doesn't really care about me.*

But as angry as he was, he knew better than that. *You'd get the trainer, then what? There are dozens of raiders between here and the exit. Dozens outside. There's a crow's nest at the top of the east horn. The odds are against you.*

Still, he wanted to test the combination. Just to know it worked.

Caleb approached the keypad on the barred cabinet. He reached for the seven. Then a long, low whistle cut the silence.

"Mustn't touch." The raider spoke with an icy edge that made Caleb's skin crawl. "I heard Ajax gave you a claw, but he didn't give you the *code*, did he?"

Caleb turned to find a man yanking the arena gate shut behind him. Dinosaur teeth circled his neck and bald scalp. He wore a dinosaur hide jacket over his bare chest, upon which three tattooed slash marks emulated scars amid the white lines of true scars.

The raider limped toward him. "Did you miss me, little boy?" He pulled one pant leg up to his thigh where a huge gouge still healed.

Caleb's eyes widened at the raider from the supply garage in Columbia—the one he'd hacked with a pickax.

"I see you finally remember old Whistler, eh?" The raider let his pant cuff fall. He chuckled.

Grumbling laughter echoed on the high ceiling of the arena.

44 chirped with alarm.

Whistler circled the arena. In the scaffolding above, more raiders gathered and watched. Dark, tattooed faces and hungry, bloodshot eyes targeted Caleb. "When I heard that the Alpha struck a deal with the little shit who killed my *Deinonychus*, who gave me this lurch in my step—you can imagine that didn't sit well with me."

Caleb gave a long sigh. He knew he should be afraid, but suddenly he was too exhausted. "*You* are my trainer?"

"Today I am." Whistler clicked the shock prod at his side, and it hummed to life.

44 growled.

"You'll find my standards a bit higher than dear departed Ajax." The raiders in the scaffolding shouted in agreement. "See, you didn't earn that mark." Whistler traced the shape of Caleb's claw tattoo over one eye. "Not really. And I'm not convinced you earned a wrist claw, either."

Whistler drew closer. Caleb tensed. 44 snarled.

"But old Whistler is a fair man. I'm willing to give you the chance to prove these honors, in front of multiple witnesses. It is my responsibility as your trainer." Whistler sneered as he passed between Caleb and the keypad to the weapons cabinet. He obscured the keys and plugged in the code, then he opened the gate and found the barbed claw that had been Caleb's. "This one's about your size, isn't it?"

"Yes," Caleb said through clenched teeth. "That one is *mine*."

Whistler's thin lips spread. "We shall see." He snapped his fingers. The arena gates burst open. More raiders spilled in. The men in the scaffolding stamped their boots on the metal. They clanged weapons against the guard rail. "Trial! Trial!" they chanted. "Trial! Trial!"

44 screeched, spread her claws, and rushed toward the first man to approach. The raider shoved a chrome shock prod into 44's stomach. Sparks flew. 44 yelped and collapsed. Her leg kicked at empty air. Her feathery tail twitched.

"Leave her alone!" Caleb raced to her side, but two raiders were already grabbing him from behind. He bit one of their hands and warm blood gushed over his tongue. He kicked and struggled.

He kneed a muscular raider in the groin. The huge man with slasher skulls curving down his biceps doubled over and squealed in agonized surprise. Caleb wrenched free from the second raider, only to find a wall of skull-faced men forming between him and 44.

Caleb shouted. A dozen raiders pointed their barbed claws in his direction. He turned to find Whistler, face twisted with malice, rushing toward him, shock prod humming up a fresh charge.

Blue sparks exploded. Electricity pulsed through Caleb's muscles. He rocketed backward. Before he could muster up an iota of energy, strong arms yanked him up. His legs hung under his limp form like cooked noodles. His arms were pulled behind him, straining the sockets at his shoulders. Coarse ropes burned at his wrists.

"Trial! Trial! Trial! Trial!" The stomping, clanking chant rattled his bones.

The rusty arena gates shrieked open, and Caleb felt himself dragged through the dust. He managed to lift his head and catch a glimpse of two giggling maniacs pulling a muzzle over 44's snout. Her gold eye darted with panic.

"Trial! Trial!"

The raiders hoisted Caleb into the air and carried him up the metal ramp. High up, the light of day, the shape of the panic gates swirled with vertigo. Claws and knives clanked. Whistler's shock prod buzzed nearby.

"Trial! Trial!"

Soon bright blue sky poured over him. High up, a *Pteranodon* circled. The raiders carried Caleb under the tunnel, through the boulder field, and they emerged between the two carnivore pens.

"Trial! Trial!" More raiders were waiting, lined on either side.

Caleb's movement was starting to return, but his arms were hopelessly pinned behind him. His captors hurled him onto the ground, and he tumbled through the gravel. He spit dust and blood, struggled to his knees, and faced the tunnel.

Whistler raised his shock prod in the air. The raiders cheered. To Caleb's right, *Deinonychuses* screeched along with the crowd. To the left, *Carnotauruses* snorted and grumbled.

Two raiders were dragging 44 through the dust. Behind the muzzle, her scarred eye was alight with fear.

Whistler cackled, did a strange little dance, and then zapped 44 on either side with his shock prod. She spasmed and plopped to one side.

Caleb screamed in protest. Whistler stepped toward Caleb and recharged his shock prod.

Caleb fell silent.

Whistler gave a knowing nod. "That's right, compound brat. Shut that screamer, because there's only one way out of this, and that's to pass your bloody trial. No help from that sack of dead meat Ajax. No help from your little runt pet. Just you and the judgement of the pack. That's the way it's supposed to be. That's the way it was for all of us!"

The crowd thundered with approval.

"What say you, men?" Whistler's voice echoed between the horns. "Trial by bull?" he produced Caleb's wrist claw and held it toward the *Carnotaurus* pen. "Or trial by slashers?" He aimed the wrist claw toward the *Deinonychus*.

The crowd unanimously agreed: "Bull! Bull! Bull! Bull!"

Sadistic euphoria lit Whistler's face. He marched to Caleb and snatched his chin. He dug dirty fingernails into Caleb's cheeks and shouted, "You want this claw?" Oniony breath steamed out.

Whistler stepped back, wound his arm, and tossed the wrist claw far over the *Carnotaurus* fence. The weapon sailed through blue sky, turned a few times, then shot down like a missile. Claw tips impaled dirt, about ten meters into the pen, between the pacing red-black bodies of hungry-looking bull-heads.

"Go fetch!" Whistler cackled.

The crowd roared. He kicked Caleb in the guts, and Caleb doubled over in pain.

"Hang on, Whistler!" a gruff voice cried out. "The boy needs his war paint."

Whistler's eyes gleamed.

44 squealed and whined.

Two raiders hoisted a barrel and carried it through the tunnel under the boulder field. They slammed it to the ground in front of Caleb. Bold black letters lined the barrel: SLURRY.

The raiders pried the lid off the barrel.

Caleb shouted as two raiders yanked him to his feet from behind and held him in place. Whistler dunked his arm up to the elbow in bloody sludge. Then he marched back to Caleb, gave a wet slap to his forehead, and smeared putrid slurry down his face.

Caleb spit. Vomit crept up his throat.

Slap! A second raider smacked Caleb's cheek and smeared slurry down his neck.

Slap! Another raider dropped a slimy hunk down the back of his vest.

The raiders lined up at the barrel, each one took a turn wetting his hand in pureed dinosaur, then approached Caleb and slathered him.

By the time they were done, his face, hair and torso were caked in slurry. Putrid red gunk was already starting to bake in the sun, to seep into his mouth, nostrils, eyes. He fought back tears. *Don't let them see you break,* he thought. *That's the last thing you have. If this is the end, then they won't get that satisfaction.*

"All right! All right! Enough!" Whistler shouted. He limped up to Caleb, sniffed his face, then made a disgusted face. "Smells like dinner!"

The crowd roared with approval.

"Open the pen!" Whistler shouted.

44 whimpered. Caleb caught a glimpse of two raiders, struggling to hold her back. The bright red plumes of her tail shook behind her. Her curved talons scraped up dust as she attempted to slash at their sturdy, industrial boots.

Bloody drips of slurry trickled behind Caleb as the raiders dragged him toward the *Carnotaurus* gate. He blocked out the rancid stench as best he could and tried to get his bearings. The claw was far from the gate, but if he ran—fast as he could—maybe he could make it before the bull-heads reached him.

The huge predators became instantly alert to the squeaking hinges of the gate. Their stout, toothy faces turned in unison on the crowd forming on either side of the opening. Caleb was dragged helplessly toward the enclosure.

Uncontrollable panic erupted inside Caleb. *I can't do this! I can't do this!* He screamed, "Help me! Please!"

Raiders laughed all around him.

"Please help!"

Who was he shouting for? His parents and Ajax were dead and gone. Ambassador Stanton was far underground under layers and layers of rock. 44 was helplessly restrained.

"You can't do this!" Caleb screamed.

Whistler shouted, "I thought the prodigy wanted a bloody claw!" He hurled another splattering of slurry from his palm onto Caleb's chest. One of the raiders stormed toward him, barbed claws raised into the air.

For a moment, Caleb thought he was going to be gutted. But instead, the men holding him spun him around. The raider cut the bonds that had pinned his arms, and then he was hoisted into the air by both arms and hurled past the open gates.

Already three horned meat-eaters were stomping in his direction. The gate slammed and rattled behind him. The pinlock scraped into place, and the raiders cheered like lunatics.

Caleb blocked out the pain in his arms and legs. He bolted alongside the interior perimeter. *Can I climb? Am I fast enough to scale the fence?*

It wasn't electrified, but he doubted he'd get high enough, fast enough. In fact, by the time a bull-head closed in, he'd end up at the perfect biting altitude.

He spotted the raider claw stuck in dirt. A *Carnotaurus* lurched between him and his weapon and roared. Yellow eyes widened under the V of the predator's horns.

Caleb pivoted. He dove and rolled in the dust just as a second *Carnotaurus* lurched from behind. The animals' snarls mixed with the crowd of roaring tormentors. Caleb had four of the five bulls on his radar—two on his left, one on his right, one lingering in observation by the rocky wall of the east horn. The wrist claw remained in biting range of the predator on his right.

What do you know about them, kid? Came Ajax's voice.

Dozens of *Carnotaurus* facts raced through Caleb's mind as he ran a wide circle to build distance.

They're big! It takes a moment for them to change directions. They have to build to a sprint.

He kept his eye on the claw as he circled.

They're not dumb, but they're not smart. Not a like a slasher.

Two bulls brushed against each other in pursuit of Caleb; one snapped at the other.

They're solitary. Not pack hunters.

Caleb changed directions. His lungs threatened to burst, but he powered on. He didn't go for the claw, where one attacker still loomed; instead, he raced toward the disinterested *Carnotaurus*—the one lingering by the wall.

That's why the raiders drug them with stimulants before a raid, he thought. *So they can unleash them—like a bomb. They don't work with bulls the same way I work with 44. They wind them up and set them loose.*

Caleb spotted the fifth *Carnotaurus*, just in time, as it lumbered around the east horn's curvature and snapped at him. He tucked and rolled. Huge three-toed feet sailed over him, scraping his elbow. The animal's massive stride completely missed him. The *Carnotaurus*'s tail whipped around, as the dinosaur awkwardly twisted to face him again.

They compete with each other! Caleb's heart throbbed. *For mates! For food!*

Before his attacker could regain his bearings, the *Carnotaurus* by the cliff charged and locked his horned head into the other's neck. They wriggled their puny arms, writhed bulky necks, and began to snap and charge at one another.

Caleb was already back on his feet. The other three bulls closed in on him. He raced for the far corner of the pen, where the three animals' girth would put them in close confines as they closed in.

The raiders' screams and jeers grew increasingly chaotic. Caleb caught glimpses of the tattooed masses over his shoulder, behind the three pursuing dinosaurs. The maniacs pressed against the fence, clanging weapons against metal support beams.

The perimeter fence partially wove into the boulder field between the horns. The rocks were too uneven for the stubby hands of a *Carnotaurus* to climb, but Caleb spotted a place where the boulders were small enough, where there were just enough grooves, that he could get a little height. If he was lucky, maybe he could even squeeze between—

Hot breath washed over him. Hard sharp objects collided with his back. The sharp tips of *Carnotaurus* horns pushed his armpits. The animal's roar vibrated the air as Caleb catapulted. He sailed toward the stack of boulders.

Time stilled and Caleb had a strange out of body feeling. He could swear he was seeing the *Carnotaurus* scooping him up, flinging him with his horns. He saw its jaws chomping the air at just the wrong angle to catch a snack. Caleb had time enough only to think to go limp.

He tumbled through dirt and gravel.

His vision spun as he struggled on rubbery knees. The *Carnotaurus* that had flung him barreled toward him.

But Caleb had been right about the space in the corner. The remaining two bull-heads encroached on either side, their eyes trained on the slurry-soaked morsel.

Caleb struggled to move, but it didn't matter. Within moments, the three *Carnotauruses* were snapping and snarling at one another, locking horns and frantically scraping against their competitors' armored hides.

He mustered every iota of will he had left and somehow managed to run. He hugged the boulder field and ducked under the swishing tails of dueling bulls.

The other two predators still fought by the cliffside. The raiders thundered with disapproval as Caleb collapsed by the barbed claw. He frantically strapped it around his wrist, glancing in both directions at the separate carnivore brawls that had broken out.

He stood unevenly and tried to get into a fighting stance. Sooner or later, one or more of these dinosaurs would dominate his rivals and come after him.

All he knew was what he'd been practicing all year: *Stick 'em under the neck.*

He clenched his fist around the handle of the claw and growled, "What's five more?"

Caleb's breath heaved. His heart felt like a bomb, too.

Kill five more carnivores. Then what?

The raiders shook the fence, screamed to the bull-heads. Chanted "Death to the compound brat!"

Then that whole crowd of savages out there…

Heavy breaths boiled out of him.

I'll kill all of them next!

A powerful horn blasted the air. The crowd instantly fell silent. Even the five *Carnotauruses* stopped fighting, and turned their scarred, devil-horned heads toward the north side of the pen.

The Alpha stood, a claw in one hand, his other hand resting on a barrel of slurry. He kicked the barrel on its side, and a putrid waterfall of entrails splattered into the food trough.

The five *Carnotauruses* became instantly disinterested in their scuffles. They thundered toward the northern perimeter, bypassing Caleb.

"Easy food up here!" the Alpha shouted at the dinosaurs. "That's right, get over here and slurp it up, savages!"

Then the Alpha pointed his claw at the crowd pressed against the fence. "And *you* savages!" his voice echoed with rage. "Do you have any idea what you've done today?"

21

The Alpha glowered down upon his raiders. The only sound was the carnotaurs, slurping at their trough. "Well?" he shouted. "What is this?"

"Justice!" Whistler cried. "Some compound brat sticks a pickax in me! Slaughters one of ours! And we reward him?"

"Survival of the fittest!" the Alpha shouted. "Let the boy out. Now!"

Caleb heard the pinlock slide up. The gate started to creak open. He raced for the exit. Part of him wanted to recoil from the pack of raiders as much as he wanted to escape the bull-heads—who had gone from savage to placid with the tilting of a barrel.

"Close the gate!" Whistler screamed. "Don't let him out!"

Caleb rushed the gate—which indeed began to close again.

"Open it!" the Alpha thundered.

The gate was half open again when Whistler stumbled forward raving. He stuck his shock prod into the chest of one of the other raiders. Sparks flew. He spun around and shocked two more raiders who had been opening the gate.

Caleb ran faster.

The Alpha roared so loud that all five *Carnotauruses* tilted their bloody snouts up in surprise.

Whistler pushed the gate shut again. Caleb charged. He pressed his full weight against it, but it clanged in place.

Whistler's dagger eyes disappeared behind the gate's metal plating. Caleb waited for the horrible sound of the security pin sliding back in, but it did not come.

Instead, the Alpha blew his horn and the crowd erupted with war cries.

Behind the gate, weapons slashed and clanked. Whistler's shock prod buzzed and popped. The crowd pressed in on the gate as a shifting, winding melee broke out.

Some shouted in support of Whistler.

Others, loyal to the Alpha, called for order as they beat at the transgressors.

And still more seemed to be giving into crazed blood lust, reaching out for the nearest opponent, hacking and screaming.

The weight of the door yanked open. Caleb glimpsed the bloody spectacle and backed away, suddenly unwilling to leave the temporary safety of the pen, where the carnotaurs had been magically tamed by the slurry trough.

He caught a glimpse of Whistler, savagely shocking the face of another raider. The victim's limbs twitched on the ground. Caleb readied his claw and continued to back away. He glanced back to make sure the carnivores remained busy at the trough. The Alpha, he noticed, had disappeared from his perch.

Amid the chaos, a streak of red feathers wove between dueling raiders. 44 slipped through the half-open gate and collided with

Caleb. He hugged and steadied her, keeping his eyes on the riot.

He worked at the muzzle. "Stay calm, girl, stay…" As he popped the strap off the muzzle, Caleb eyed her swishy, bushy tail-feathers, distressed and bristled in the commotion. She had been through hell, just like him—but maybe there was opportunity in this hell.

"Stay still," he whispered. He slid off the muzzle.

44 stretched her jaws and unleashed an agonized screech.

"I know, girl. I'm sorry." Caleb unstrapped his claw. None of the battling raiders were paying attention. He carefully strapped his wrist claw around the thick middle of 44's tail, securing it between ruffled feathers.

44 grunted in distress and started to twist around. Caleb pressed her back down with one hand and stroked her. "Please! Please, sit still. Just a second. Come on, 44."

She whined and chirped. Caleb tightened the straps of the weapon. The handle hooked underneath, holding the claw in place. The barbed blades curved backwards, between ruffled red quills. Caleb could see the razor edges, but dust had dulled the metallic gleam.

He stroked 44's feathers. He glanced back at the trough. One of the five bulls eyed him and 44 with a sloppy red snout, then lazily dunked his head back down for more slurry.

The riot raged on, and the raiders disbursed between the two animal pens. Nobody was guarding the gate now. Caleb cautiously led 44 toward the opening.

The Alpha's horn cut the air. Most of the raiders ceased their battle at the sound. But Whistler and his followers continued to assault their opponents.

Caleb and 44 crept into the clearing. Caleb shoved the gate closed. He found the metal pin and slid it back through, securing the *Carnotaurus* pen.

"Who started this!" the Alpha demanded.

One by one, the Alpha's followers began to point their weapons at Whistler and his friends. Several raiders lay bleeding out on the ground. Whistler and his crew backed up into the center, perfectly between the *Deinonychus* and *Carnotaurus* enclosures.

The Alpha strode up to them. "You do *not* incite war within our pack, Whistler! If you have a challenge—" he pounded his chest, pointed his claws at the man's eyes— "you challenge *me*!"

Caleb's mind raced. *Is this the time to slip away? Or will this be over before I can get to the keys and steal a jeep?*

And then there was Ambassador Stanton, of course. Working underground. Oblivious to Caleb's suffering, like he had been before all of this started.

"There will be no challenge now!" The Alpha declared. "Whistler must die! And if you stand by him, you too will die."

The small crowd of men around Whistler exchanged uneasy glances. One by one, they walked forward and knelt before the Alpha.

A young man with buzzed red hair and *Deinonychus* tattoos bowed before the Alpha. "I beg your pardon. I had failed to think of the pack, and I submit myself for punishment."

The Alpha punched this man on the jaw with his non-clawed fist. A tooth flew from the penitent man's jaw and landed with a sprinkle of blood in the dust.

The next traitor knelt before the Alpha. "I beg your pardon. I had failed to think of the pack, and I submit myself for punishment."

"You cowards!" Whistler screamed. "Where is the justice? The law of the pack! The Alpha thinks only of himself!"

Caleb glanced in every direction. The ranks of men and women loyal to the Alpha now blocked the tunnel back to the vehicle lot. He would have to circle the horns the long way to escape. It was too risky.

The Alpha struck each man in turn who confessed their transgression and allowed them to fold back into the crowd. Then the Alpha snapped his fingers. Two burly raiders wrangled Whistler and stripped him of his weapons.

"Cowards!" Whistler writhed and shouted. "Cowards!"

They brought Whistler before the Alpha. The Alpha removed his claw and proceeded to beat Whistler with bare fists. Blood spurted from Whistler's lips with every smack. Whistler hung from the arms of the two raiders.

"Caleb!" the Alpha shouted.

The men turned Whistler's broken, bloody body toward Caleb and 44.

"You have been wronged by this member of our pack!" the Alpha thundered. "His punishment is death. You have the right to slay him."

Tears burned in Caleb's eyes. He shook his head. His voice broke. "I don't want to."

The Alpha glared in disapproval. "You started this. You wounded Whistler in Columbia. That wound festered within him. Now you refuse to put him out of his misery?"

Caleb spat. "They're *your* pack! You do it."

The Alpha snapped his fingers and pointed toward the feeding platform. Whistler's mumbling laughter echoed as the two men carried him away.

The Alpha approached Caleb and lowered his voice. "I am going to let that disrespect slide today, Caleb, not because you have been through anything I don't expect a member of my pack to survive—but purely because your father has promised to do me the courtesy of a favor. Remember that."

The Alpha marched after the two men who were dragging Whistler toward the feeding platform.

Whistler screamed as he was hoisted to the top of the platform, above the slurping, chomping line of *Carnotauruses*.

"This place is a joke!" Whistler cackled. "This world is a joke! A cruel joke!"

The men held him at the edge of the platform. The Alpha climbed up and strapped his claw back on. "You think this is funny, Whistler?"

Whistler laughed harder.

The Alpha stabbed Whistler in the guts and yanked his claw back out. Entrails rained over the feasting carnivores. Two of them glanced up as fresh blood dribbled into the trough.

"Laugh it up!" The Alpha shoved Whistler over the edge. Before he hit ground, the two interested bull-heads each snatched one end.

With a graceful twist of their snouts, they tore Whistler's body apart at the waist and munched contentedly on either half.

Once again, a surreal sensation came over Caleb, like he was watching himself, outside of his own body. Two raiders silently marched him and 44 back through the tunnel. He recoiled and sobbed as they neared the entrance under the horns. He wanted nothing less than to go back underground.

His attendants brought him to the showers and allowed him a chance to scrub as much slurry off his body as possible. He snuck nervous glances at 44, curled underneath a locker room bench.

Neither raider seemed to notice the irregularity where he had hidden the wrist claw in her ruffled, dust-caked feathers.

Caleb was not presented with clean clothes, so he didn't bother to put the slurry-stained shirt and vest back on. He marched wearily back to his and Stanton's cell, where the raiders instructed him to "Sleep off the day."

And he did sleep—a long troubled sleep where hungry bull-heads circled his mother. In the dream, he struggled to save her. The closer he got, the slower his body moved. Like his arms and legs were made of stone.

He saw his father, dressed in the sleek gray attire of a compound representative—as he had first met Ambassador Stanton. And his father told him that while he *could* help Caleb get out of this nightmare, he had no desire to and never would.

He saw Ajax, gutted by the Alpha and tossed into the slurry.

He saw sparks sputtering from a thousand shock prods. Electricity coursed through 44's lithe body. Her gold eye rolled behind the scar that mirrored Caleb's tattoo.

When he woke, Ambassador Stanton was there, with tears in his eyes. The raiders had allowed him to bring a tin cup of water and a strip of jerky form the mess hall, but that was all.

Caleb did not speak to Ambassador Stanton, but he guzzled most of the water and devoured half the jerky. He gave the rest to 44.

"Caleb," Stanton said calmly. "I know this is hard. But you have to talk to me. I need to know you're okay."

Caleb opened his mouth, not sure what to say.

I am okay.

I'm not okay.

I hate your guts.

I hate everyone's guts.

But he surprised himself when all that came out was a lunatic laugh, like Whistler's. Terror trembled through him. *Maybe I am turning into one of them after all.*

"Caleb," Ambassador Stanton said. "Please. Talk to me."

Caleb laughed and laughed until his aching sides ached even more.

44 purred with concern.

"Caleb." Stanton cautiously placed his hands on his shoulders. "Look at me. Please. Why are you laughing?"

"Because," came Caleb's hoarse whisper. He reached and slowly unhooked the claw from 44's tail. It dropped onto the cot with a puff of desert dust.

"I got us a weapon."

22

The next morning, Necra opened their cell door. "Follow me. The boy is to report to the arena."

Stanton crossed his arms. "No."

Necra's eyes widened.

Stanton shrugged. "No."

"You have no choice in this."

"My son has been traumatized," Stanton said. "He stays here. For at least another day."

Necra glared at Caleb. "Report to the arena."

"I demand to speak to the Alpha," Stanton said. "He guaranteed that my son would be treated with respect. Caleb is the sole reason I am cooperating with you people. This is a serious violation of our pact."

"Your son will wait in the arena!" Necra shouted. "The Alpha will speak with you when he—"

"Listen, you psychopath!" Stanton raised his voice even louder.

Necra startled in surprise.

"Dad, stop!" Caleb's voice remained scratchy with exhaustion. "I'll go. It's okay."

"It's *not* okay!" Stanton thundered.

"Please." Caleb got between him and Necra. He hugged Stanton.

Stanton hugged him back, tears brimmed under his eyes. It was a scripted moment between himself and Caleb, of course. They'd plotted half the night about the next twenty-four hours. Nevertheless, Stanton had come to care for Caleb, and for him at least, the hug was real.

"Go with Necra," Caleb whispered. "Cooperate. We just want this to be over, right?"

"I don't want you out there with them," Stanton said. "I want you with me."

"44 needs the exercise anyway," Caleb said. "They're not going to give me another trainer like Whistler. I think the Alpha knows that was a mistake."

Necra leaned against the doorway. "Are you two quite finished? Follow me!"

Stanton returned Necra's carnivorous glare. She twisted around and struck a path toward the nexus of the cave system. "Follow!" her voice echoed.

Stanton nodded at Caleb. They followed Necra through the main hub. Caleb didn't even wait for Necra's instructions, he just beckoned 44 to follow him into the arena, where Stanton assumed the Alpha himself was waiting, or would soon show up to train Caleb, as he had promised—or perhaps threatened—to do.

Stanton assumed Whistler had been instructed to push Caleb's training as a means of psychological torment. The Alpha probably had disliked that Ajax had bonded with him, but underestimated Whistler's bitterness. Stanton truly suspected the Alpha did not intend for Caleb's torment to go that far.

Traumatic as it was, now that the incident had happened, it was leverage: their last, best chance to get out alive.

Necra led him all the way to her bio-chemistry lab. A crate of supplies waited on the lab table, the very same spot where Ajax's life had slipped away.

Necra slapped the side of the crate. "Sort this." She started to busy herself at the counter.

"No."

She turned and glared.

Stanton crossed his arms. "No."

"Do your job!"

"I demand to speak to him."

"You demand nothing of the Alpha or of me!"

"You are not in charge, Necra. He is in charge. He is responsible for what happens to my son. And he almost got him killed. What am I supposed to do now? You don't speak for him. I need to see him. Right now!"

Necra slammed her fists on the table between them. "You make no demands!"

Stanton yelled, "Today I do!"

For a brief moment, Necra shrank back in surprise.

"You slathered my son in putrid animal slurry—that for all I know was infected with your bull-fever. Then you shoved him into—"

"Your son is *not* infected! We are very careful with—"

"Of *course* you are!" Stanton slammed his own fists down.

"Because you'd never deliberately harm one of your horrible pets! A human child, by all means! Shock prod him and throw him to the carnivores!"

"Whistler has been punished!"

"But Caleb has not recovered. He has shock burns. His clothes are stained with blood. He's exhausted, malnourished. He gave half the scrap of food you let us have in our cell last night to his mangy pet. A dumb slasher that you people brainwashed him into loving!"

Necra laughed. "Is it so horrible that we gave your son a pet?"

"He needs food! He needs a solid meal. Right now!"

"I am not a chef, and it is not dinner time!"

Stanton gave a wild, angry laugh. "I'm expected to abandon my son here and go poison an entire city to ensure his safety. But you people can't even guarantee his safety while I'm still *among* you! Why ever would I leave him here?"

Necra glared.

"Fetch the Alpha," Stanton snapped.

"If you make one more demand of me," Necra's voice dropped to a chill whisper, "I will gouge out your eyes and devour them."

"Necra." Stanton evened out his tone. "I don't care how much you hate me. You *can't* kill me. I'm essential to your plan."

"You are a far greater liability than an asset, Ambassador Stanton. Perhaps the Alpha has not fully seen it yet, but I do."

"It burns you up, doesn't it?" Stanton whispered. "Now that your virus has been manufactured, the Alpha needs me even more than he needs you."

Necra screeched and leapt over the table. In a heartbeat, she tackled Stanton to the floor, knocking the supply crate over. Metal instruments clattered around them. She clenched his throat.

Stanton choked and struggled to alleviate the pressure of her vice-like grip.

"It is *you* and your pathetic child who are expendable, Niles Stanton!" she hissed. "We could dispose of you right now, and all we'd need to do is watch and wait and pluck another willing Triassican from the road. There are a hundred cowards behind those walls who would sacrifice your whole city to save themselves or someone they love. That is the terrible truth that you will now learn when it is too late."

Stanton struggled to speak.

"When we take the mining town, it will be even easier. That's the way we *should* do it! That's the way we *would* have done it. First Columbia, *then* Triassica. And if you and your boy had not shown up when you did—"

Stanton grabbed Necra's face. He shoved his thumbs into her eyes. The woman instantly released her grip on his neck. She squirmed away before he could apply pressure. Stanton snatched the back of her neck.

"You're wrong!" He pushed forward and clocked her head against the corner of the examining table.

Necra screamed in surprise.

"Your virus is canned and ready to go!" Stanton hurled her to the floor and stood over her. "Your boss needs *me*! Not you!"

A crimson gash slashed the *Pteranodon* beak on her forehead. Her eyes quivered with shock.

"Am I speaking your language yet, Necra!" Stanton shouted. "Go! Get! The Alpha!"

Necra backed away and flipped to her feet in one fluid motion.

"Go!" Stanton screamed.

Blood oozed down the *Pteranodon* tattoo, past her mouth. Necra shook her head and exited the lab. Her boots clanked up the metal steps.

Stanton trembled, but wasted no time. He opened the cabinet and grabbed the medical tape, then he unlocked the fridge and gathered the carnivore stimulants along with a few empty syringes. He carefully strapped the syringes and vials of stimulants to his back, rounded the tape several more times, then covered them with his shirt and vest.

The tape would have to hold possibly all day, or at least until he could find an opportunity to stash them near the vet bay.

He quickly examined the contents of the spilled crate: scalpels, needles, gauze, and other medical supplies. He reached for a scalpel, just as the Alpha's heavy boots came clanking down the steps. Stanton tossed the medical tape in the pile of spilled supplies.

The Alpha emerged with his usual stoic expression. "You have a grievance, Ambassador Stanton?"

"That is a serious understatement."

"You clocked Necra pretty hard," the Alpha said. "You're lucky she didn't kill you."

"I think she knows, like we know, that we all need each other. And you're smart enough to realize that after yesterday, there is a big problem with all of that."

The Alpha nodded. "I will train Caleb myself going forward."

"That's not much of a comfort."

"Hm." The Alpha glanced at the spilled crate. "Would you mind cleaning that up?"

"Yes, I would," Stanton said. "My son needs a meal."

"We do not eat when we choose in my pack. We eat at the appointed time."

"He's not one of you," Stanton snapped. "He's my son. Feed him!"

"You've got an attitude today, Ambassador," The Alpha said coolly. "And I hope you can appreciate my own diplomacy this morning. I'll have you know that I recognized Caleb's fatigue, and when Necra relayed your complaints, I asked her to escort Caleb to the mess hall for an unscheduled breakfast."

Stanton took a shaky breath.

"He is eating as we speak."

"Thank you."

"Whistler did not carry out those actions under my orders," the Alpha explained. "I had assigned Whistler's buddy Jaggo to be Caleb's trainer. Jaggo died in the scuffle yesterday before I could punish him for allowing Whistler to do what he did."

Stanton glared.

"What more can I tell you to put your mind at ease?"

Stanton continued to say nothing.

"I would like for us to go back to putting our plans into motion, Ambassador Stanton."

"I can't leave Caleb after what happened." Stanton shrugged. "I just can't."

The Alpha raised an eyebrow. "Okay. Shall I kill you and Caleb today, then? Have I wasted my time?"

"Make me your hostage. Send Caleb back with the virus. That I could live with."

The Alpha gave a grim hum and shook his head. "Now, Ambassador, I know that you would simply tell your son to let us kill you. You would not place that burden of mass murder on your boy. To save him, though, I do believe you would do it yourself."

"I would do anything for him."

"You know it's funny," the Alpha said. "I was beginning to wonder about you two. But now I hear it in your voice. You *would* do anything for him. I believe you."

"I *can't* leave him. I can't let this training continue. If it was still Ajax…"

"There are no more Whistlers lurking under this horn, Ambassador Stanton. That was an oversight of mine. I apologize."

"You? Apologize?" Stanton shook his head. "Well… I guess I am speechless."

"Caleb can rest today. And you would best keep your distance from Necra," the Alpha said. "She *will* try to kill you. And I like you, Niles Stanton. I don't want you dead. Not until our business has concluded and you are a contented grandfather, far, far away from here. I'm sure you like that idea. I like it too."

Stanton nodded.

"There is a future for you and your son. It will not involve compounds or savages or monsters. Just you and him, some quiet place where you go and work that silver tongue of yours to build a nice, safe life, away from all this conflict. You deserve that. So does your boy."

"Thank you," Stanton whispered.

"But if you fail me, I will rip your heart out and give it to Necra as a peace offering."

"I understand," Stanton said. "With all due respect, I sense your sincerity, but you haven't given me any new assurances. Caleb gets to eat and rest today, but how and why should I ever expect to find him alive after I've done your favor?"

"I can send him west. The training camp would have no idea he's a compound brat. They would treat him like anyone else, so long as he keeps his head down."

Stanton let out a long, anguished breath. The medical tape itched his chest.

"I know your father's heart aches to hear that he's going to be even further away, but what else can I do? He's *my* leverage, Ambassador. He's all I got. That, or kill you both."

"Okay," Stanton shrugged. "I suppose that's good enough for now."

"I'll send someone to take you back to your cell," The Alpha said. "You don't want to be here when Necra returns."

"One more thing," Stanton said.

The Alpha arched his eyes. "Yes?"

"I've been thinking about my return to Triassica. How it will work. We'll have to design something to hold the virus. Those cannisters are too suspicious."

"We'll work that out," the Alpha said.

"The best way to go about it is to let me return without the virus in hand. Wait two weeks for me to grieve the loss of my son publicly, then I'll do a job for the council, and we can rendezvous and hide the virus in my luggage. They never search me. The timetable will be longer than I'd like it to be, but we can't rush this job."

The Alpha placed his hand on Stanton's shoulder. "You're right. You've been right about a lot since I brought you here. I'm glad you're giving this careful thought."

"It won't be easy."

The Alpha smiled. "It's going to work, and when it's all over, not only will you have your son back, but I may even reward you."

"Do you have paper? Can I bring paper and pen back to my room? I'd like to start plotting this. I want to get it over with."

The Alpha crossed the lab, rummaged through a supply drawer, and tossed a pad of paper and a charcoal pencil onto the metal table. "Get to work."

23

That evening, Stanton and Caleb reported to the Alpha's table for dinner. Caleb kept his head down, while Stanton shared pages of hand drawn maps and information.

He had spent most of the day constructing a breakdown of Triassica, including the filtration compound, a rough mockup of the sewer system, and the terrain north of the mountain gate where he proposed a rendezvous to pick up the virus.

He even drafted a rough narrative about how he had lost his son while trying to survive in the raiders' territory. The Alpha smiled when he read the part about how Caleb had failed to spot an invasive dryptosaur.

"I like that," the Alpha said. "A touch of reality lends credibility."

Caleb snuck furtive glances at the line of raiders filling their mugs at the mead casks. The Alpha had set up not one, but two barrels that day. Stanton suspected the extra booze was a means of dulling any lingering rebellious spirits after Whistler's punishment.

He keeps them drunk. He keeps them happy. He keeps them on his program, Stanton thought. As per usual, the Alpha himself drank only water.

The Alpha folded Stanton's plans and tucked them into his vest pocket. "I appreciate your detailed thoughts on our operation."

Stanton nodded. "We want this to go smoothly. It's in everyone's interest." Lately the Alpha had been eerily apologetic and respectful. *Either he's getting ready to finally kill us, or my tirade in the lab truly forced him to take some of the pressure off.*

"You and Caleb have the option of taking a personal day tomorrow. You can stay in your cell or take a walk around the horns—supervised of course," the Alpha said.

"If it's okay," Caleb spoke up. "I want to resume my training. 44 was learning a lot with Ajax's help. I think we got interrupted."

The Alpha gave an impressed smile. "You're right. It would be good to get her back on a program. Gives you something to do, too." He glanced at Stanton. "How about it, Ambassador? Would you care to observe your son's training tomorrow?"

"I heard a lot about the good work that Ajax did with Caleb," Stanton said. "I'm eager to see that work continue."

"Ajax was good." The Alpha took a bite of *Deinonychus* jerky. "Of course, there's no better animal whisperer under the horn than Necra."

Stanton checked the food and mead line. He scoured the tables and the entranceway, but Necra had not shown up for dinner.

"However, as your relationship with Necra now requires mending, it makes no sense to put her in charge of Caleb." The Alpha smiled.

"Necra's skillset should be applied toward the plan in your pocket," Stanton said. "I still have a lot to learn from her, about the handling and disbursement of her… creation."

The Alpha finished his meal and leaned back in satisfaction. "I'm happy with how our arrangement has progressed."

Stanton nodded.

"We've certainly had our moments. All of us," the Alpha said. "But we're in a good place now."

The Alpha clapped his hands. He stood and blew his horn. The hall grew dead quiet. Everyone turned toward the man with the *Carnotaurus* face.

"My pack!" the Alpha thundered. "Listen well! We have much to celebrate. And I am pleased to announce the promise of an even stronger tomorrow for the men and women who tame the most terrible beasts in New Pangea!"

A raucous chorus filled the hall. The raiders clinked their mugs and slugged frothy beverages.

As the shouting died down, the Alpha resumed. "You all know our guests, Ambassador Stanton and his son Caleb. I want to remind you all that Caleb, thanks to his earnest devotion to his training, as well as a multitude of impressive feats, including a true and swift bond with his animal, must be treated and respected as one of us. As a brother—in training, still—but a brother nonetheless."

A somewhat less enthusiastic round of cheers grumbled from surrounding tables.

Caleb blanched and lowered his face.

Just paint a target on his back, why don't you? Stanton thought.

"Caleb's father too is a true ally to our people. He has provided valuable information and pledged himself to a plan that will gain us access not only to the mining town of Columbia, but ultimately to the very gateway to southern lands."

An awed hush came over the crowd.

"You heard correctly," the Alpha said. "I promise you—men, women, and beasts—the great fortress of Triassica, by year's end, perhaps sooner, will belong to us. Facilities, resources, medicine, knowledge more valuable than any mine." His inky smile spread. "Weapons that can punch a hole through a rex. All thanks to Ambassador Stanton!"

The Alpha raised his canteen. "On this night, we thank him, for all that he has done for us so far, and for all that he *will* do for our future! Here! Here!"

The raiders cried out with newfound enthusiasm. They clanked mugs, chugged, shouted, screamed, and chattered in bemused voices, demanding more information about this fantastical plan.

The Alpha lowered his arms. "Those of you who shall play a part will learn more in coming days and weeks. The risk to us is small. We will strike not with an army, but a venomous sting. They will not see us coming. They will never learn who ended them. But their neighbors—Jurassica, Cretacia, and everything between—will cower in our shadow!"

The Alpha reached across the table and clapped Stanton's shoulder. "And this man will make it happen! Three cheers for Niles Stanton!"

"Stanton! Stanton!" a small pack of raiders started to stomp boots and clank cutlery. "Stanton! Stanton!" More and more raiders cheered his name.

Stanton nodded respectfully as he turned in acknowledgement. Caleb glared at his plate; the boy could not repress a scowl. Stanton touched his "son's" arm and whispered reassurance—loud enough so the Alpha could hear over the din. "It's okay, Caleb. From now on, we'll be okay."

Caleb gave a weak nod and wiped a tear from one eye.

One table of raiders broke into song:

Crash the walls!
Stick the guards!
Snag their goods!
Hit 'em hard!
Bulls on the battlefront!
Slashers past the gates!
Weaklings stomped!
That's their fate!
Triassica! Triassica!
Raze it to the ground!
Leave 'em good and dead,
And starving all year round!

Caleb scowled harder, and Stanton suddenly realized the boy had heard this song before. He glanced up at the Alpha, who seemed to read his mind.

"This song is usually about Columbia." The Alpha guzzled his water. "They'll have to come up with a new one. Nobody in Triassica is going to starve."

Triassica! Triassica!
Leave 'em good and dead!

Slashers get their guts,
And bulls snap off their heads!
Triassica! Triassica!
Cemetery plots!
Fliers pick 'em over,
While their children lay and rot!

Stanton surveyed the mess hall. Every raider sang, laughed, and smiled hideous tattooed faces. They were returning eagerly to the double casks of mead for seconds.

Caleb was struggling to maintain his composure. Had they sung this song after he lost his real father and mother?

The Alpha made eye contact and nodded toward Caleb's red-faced scowl.

"I'm sorry." Stanton spoke in the same apologetic tone he had used to present Triassica's refusal to the Triumvirate, only a few short weeks back. "This is difficult for him."

The Alpha folded his arms.

"Caleb," Stanton said, in a stern, fatherly tone. "Finish your dinner and thank the Alpha for his many kind concessions. Then…" He glanced back up at the Alpha. "If it's permitted… we would be happy to retire early."

The Alpha nodded. "That is acceptable."

The song about Triassica looped back to the verse about "crashing the walls" and "sticking the guards." Some raiders, in drunken habit, were now indeed singing about Columbia. Half the crowd promised to bring the mining town to ruin, the other half the compound.

Caleb ate in silence. Stanton hurried to finish the pasty gray gruel and strip of jerky on his own tray.

The Alpha appointed a tipsy, twenty-something raider—with a hook for a hand and a *Carnotaurus* footprint on his bare chest—to escort them to their cell. The feast raged on. The song about Columbia/Triassica echoed through the caverns as they traversed dim passages.

Caleb and Stanton drew back a few paces as the raider stumbled through the tunnel to their room. Stanton nodded to Caleb. The boy was smiling now.

They reached the metal door of their cell. The raider unlocked it and started to open it.

Stanton banged his forehead against the metal frame.

The raider shouted. He spun and slashed his hook. Stanton sidestepped and caught the Raider's wrist; the tip of the hook whooshed centimeters from his neck. Before the raider made another move, Caleb dove for his legs. The raider tripped into the half-open doorway. He reached for Caleb, but a feathery snout shot through the door. Reptilian claws grabbed the raider's shoulder and pulled him down.

The raider shrieked as 44 gnawed his neck. "You sons of—" Caleb kicked the man's groin, and he unleashed an agonized yelp.

"Back, 44!" Caleb commanded.

The *Deinonychus* withdrew into the room, leaving the raider's head positioned between the doorframe. Stanton cracked the door against the raider's skull.

The man went limp. His hook clanged against stone. Blood

pooled under his head.

"Hurry." Stanton pulled the door open wide again.

Caleb rushed inside and rubbed 44's snout affectionately. "Good girl! Good girl!" He reached into a slit that had been carefully cut into the base of his cot's mattress and removed his smuggled wrist claw, which he swiftly fastened to his right hand.

"Be very, very careful with that," Stanton warned.

"I know how to use this," Caleb said.

"I know you do, but still."

Caleb nodded. "Yeah… I know."

Stanton rummaged into his own mattress and found three prepared syringes of *Carnotaurus* stimulant. He stowed them in his vest pocket and then placed a hand on Caleb's shoulder. "Caleb, you know I couldn't be sorrier about all this, right?"

He nodded.

"One way or another—I promise you—it's almost over. You're getting out."

"I hope so. I hope we both do." He ran his fingers through 44's red feathers. "But I already got something I wanted."

Caleb and Stanton crept toward the hub of the cave system. They waited by the opening. Caleb hushed 44. Twelve drunken raiders made their way toward the freight elevator to relieve the outside sentry crew.

"We've got minutes before the sentries up there return for the end of dinner," Stanton whispered. "Let's hit the arena, but make it fast. We have to get to the examining pens without getting spotted."

They hurried through the hub toward the arena. The raiders' war songs rumbled from the mess hall on the other side of the pillar. Caleb and 44 kicked up dust as they rushed toward the weapons case.

The boy punched in Ajax's code and slid the gate open. He reached for an iron hunting knife with a dinosaur bone handle. Then he procured a holster for his claw and carefully stowed that weapon.

Stanton breathed a sigh of relief to see the barbed tips secured, rather than waving about.

The boy handed Stanton a large hunting knife with a serrated base. The weapon reminded Stanton of the blade his brother Clint had used to carve *Dimetrodon* sails from the animals' backs.

Stanton scanned the racks of weapons. Most of them were too heavy or cumbersome to do them any good. But he spotted something else: a coil of nylon rope, not long, but enough to come in handy. "Hand me that rope, Caleb," he said. "Then we'd better move."

Caleb passed Stanton the rope, then frantically searched the racks. "We need a shock prod. I'm not sure how we'll do this without one."

"I don't see one," Stanton said. "They must be all checked out or at the top of the elevator shaft. Maybe there's one in vet bay."

"What if there isn't?"

"We'll have to chance it. We can't risk trying to take one off a raider."

They left the arena and paused again at the nexus. The relieved shift ambled into the mess hall. They greeted their pack by belting into a song about "life being good under the horns."

"How could life be good here?" Caleb whispered. "Half these freaks tried to mutiny just yesterday."

44 seemed to chitter in agreement.

"The Alpha knows how to manipulate their loyalty," Stanton whispered. "Threat of violence. Get the booze flowing. Unite them with the promise of a common cause. It's pack mentality."

"It's sick," Caleb whispered.

"It doesn't have to be," Stanton said. "It just… is… this time."

After the new arrivals dispersed into the mess hall, the singing grew louder. Stanton nodded to Caleb. "Keep low," he mouthed.

They hurried left, through the wide, winding tunnel that skirted the edges of the horn. Stanton's heart pounded. *If this doesn't work, if we get stuck back here, that's it*, he thought. *Past the vet bay there's nothing but the elevator to the top and Necra's lab. The only exits are splattering on the rocks or drinking what's locked in the freezer.*

So far, every time he'd passed the vet bay, at least two bull-heads were locked up in each pen. If that didn't hold true tonight, they were even more out of luck.

He breathed a sigh of relief when he heard the snorts of a captive *Carnotaurus* echoing down the wide curve.

They approached and ducked behind a crate from Columbia. 44 slipped behind Caleb like his feathery red shadow. The vet bay was dark, but appeared to be empty. One pen in the row contained the shifting snout of a four-meter-tall beast.

"One *Carnotaurus*." Stanton cautiously slipped from behind the crate, once he was sure nobody was lurking. "That makes our job easier, but will it be enough of a distraction?"

Caleb hurried toward the examining tables and supply cabinets; 44 scampered after him. "Nothing about this will be easy if we can't find a shock prod." He groaned in frustration. "I don't see one!"

Stanton glanced over his shoulder, fearing a sentry could stumble upon them any minute, but it remained clear. He approached the gate and examined the huge golden eye of the caged predator.

The beast snarled. Her breath reeked of rotten meat.

"There's got to be another way to subdue or stun them, right?" Stanton removed one syringe from his pocket; the needle was long, secured with a protective cap. He wasn't totally sure what the right dosage would be, so he'd made an educated guess and evenly distributed the vial among all three shots.

"I've never seen them wrangle one without a shock prod," Caleb said. "They're big, and sometimes they're clumsy, but these cells are too small. If we stick it in the wrong place, or at the wrong angle, we'll lose an arm."

The animal's nostrils flared; her eyes widened, and she shifted her snout. A low growl rumbled in her throat.

"Hm." Stanton glanced at Caleb who continued to hunt under the examining table for a shock prod. Stanton eyed the red stains on the boy's clothes. "I think our bull smells something."

Caleb glanced up. 44 gave a confused chirp.

"Hand me your vest, Caleb."

Caleb removed his unwashed raider vest. Dried slurry remained caked into the fabric. Stanton bunched the vest up with one hand and held it to one side of the *Carnotaurus* pen. The bull grunted and swayed her head left to follow the slurry scent. "Smells like food, doesn't it?"

Caleb smiled.

Stanton handed him the syringe. "I'll climb the gate and hold this vest up as high as I can. You scale that side." He pointed right. "When she cranes her face toward me, stick her in the soft tissue around the eye socket or the side of her mouth."

"You sure about this?" Caleb said. "If you lose a hand…"

"If anything happens to me, you keep going. Promise?"

Caleb nodded.

"Okay. Give me a moment, let her get a fix on me, then sneak to the other side." Stanton held the vest in his left hand and started to climb the bars to the left of the pen. The *Carnotaurus* immediately grumbled in hunger and started chomping her stubby snout at the corner. Stanton kept the vest just out of reach, but it was hard to climb one-handed.

He winced as *Carnotaurus* breath soured over his face. The rough, wet surface of a groping predator's tongue slathered past his fingers, and he nearly let go.

Caleb was already halfway up. Stanton reached eye-level with the bull. The animal pressed her head against the gates. The metal trembled at the force of her neck and shoulder muscles, but the gate—thankfully—was designed to hold. Stanton leaned back as far as he could, the tips of the bull's horns poked toward his face. The animal snarled.

Caleb hung to the right, one hand hooked dangerously inside the bars as he used his teeth to remove the cap from the syringe. He leaned forward to make an injection in what Stanton could only guess was the predator's eye.

Suddenly the beast lurched backward. The gate rattled. She head-butted the bars. Caleb dropped the needle inside the pen.

They both stumbled and grabbed the bars for support. Stanton's legs hung in midair. Caleb was groping forward, hooking more of his slender arm through the gap.

"Caleb! Drop!" Stanton shouted.

He released—moments before the *Carnotaurus* snapped where his hand would have been. The boy hit the rock with a thud. 44 rushed to his side, sniffing with concern.

The *Carnotaurus* rammed the gate again. Stanton let go, tucked, and rolled to break his fall. The slurry-stained vest fell at the foot of the gate. He got to his feet and groaned. "You all right?"

"Fine," Caleb whispered. He sat up and rubbed his shoulder. The syringe now lay a few centimeters inside the pen. "Sorry."

"It's okay." Stanton produced another stimulant shot. "We've got two more shots."

"You have no more shots," came Necra's voice.

Volts of pain coursed through Stanton's muscles. Blue flashes sparked around him.

He keeled over. A burning stench lingered. His shoulder blazed with pain.

Necra loomed over him, face twisted with malice; a large gash remained on her forehead and a purple bruise bulged on her cheek.

Stanton's limbs twitched. The bull-head's serrated teeth smiled through the bars behind Necra.

"I am going to slaughter your son like a farm animal." She recharged her shock prod with a musical hum. "Right before your eyes!"

25

Caleb was barely back on his feet by the time Necra slipped from the shadows, as invisibly as a dryptosaur. Before he could open his mouth, she'd stunned Ambassador Stanton and kicked him toward the animal pen.

"I am going to slaughter your son like a farm animal. Right before your eyes!"

Caleb drew his father's knife. Necra rushed him. A two-pronged wrist claw poked from her right knuckles like wasp stingers. He slashed up and deflected her claw.

She thrust her humming shock prod at Caleb's side, but 44's jaws clamped her wrist and yanked her away. She grimaced, twirled the shock prod like a baton, and in a split moment, flipped the charged tip.

"44, let go!" Caleb shouted.

Blue sparks flashed. 44 yelped and released her jaws, leaving bloody toothmarks in Necra's flesh.

Caleb reached for the handle of Necra's shock prod, but she was already slashing at him again with her right hand. He backed up and pointed his knife forward.

Necra's shock prod hummed. She crouched and circled Caleb,

eyes blazing with menace. "It is not fair that you should pay for your father's sins. I would not have wished this upon you."

"You would have tossed me in the slurry if you didn't need him," Caleb growled between clenched teeth. "You don't think I remember that?"

Nearby, the captive *Carnotaurus* growled.

"I sense savagery in you, boy." Necra grinned.

Behind her, 44's clawed foot twitched. Ambassador Stanton groaned in pain.

"You are better than that man," Necra said. "There was a time when my pack saved me from a terrible destiny, chosen by *my* father. I offer you that same salvation."

Caleb tightened his grip on his real father's blade. "It's too late for your pack."

"It is not too late for you," Necra said. "Kill your father. Join us."

Before he could answer, Necra thrust her shock prod forward. A node of electricity flashed.

Caleb pivoted and brought his blade down at her. She blocked with her claw. Metal clashed and scraped. She thrust her shock prod again.

This time, Caleb dropped to his knees, tilted backward, and slashed the air above him, carving Necra's fingers. She dropped the shock-prod.

Before it hit ground, Caleb caught it and hurled it across the vet bay. "44, fetch!"

Necra thrust barbed prongs downward, but 44's clawed hands grabbed her shoulders. The feathery red streak pulled Necra backward and leapt over her. Necra stumbled back, disoriented.

Caleb charged her. He hacked. His blade scraped down her claws and cut into her knuckles. She snarled, grabbed Caleb's shirt, and slammed him into one of the examining tables.

She hissed and reared her claws back to gut him.

But 44 was already rocketing back, the metal rod secured in her jaws.

Caleb blocked Necra's claws with his father's knife. He reached and accepted the handle of the shock prod from his slasher. In one fluid motion, Caleb hit the trigger and jammed it into Necra's stomach.

Another blue-white flash seared his vision. Necra flew backward. Miraculously she stayed on two feet, but she was groping at the air in front of her, momentarily blinded. Caleb charged her. He shoved Necra toward the *Carnotaurus* pen. She reached her arm out to stop herself from colliding into the gate—instead, it shot right through a gap in the bars.

The *Carnotaurus* chomped over Necra's outstretched hand.

Stanton struggled to his feet.

Necra's screams prickled Caleb's eardrums. *If the other raiders didn't hear this disturbance,* he thought, *they will now.*

Caleb used all his strength to keep Necra pressed against the bars. Had she not been in tremendous pain, he knew, he could never have held her. When he glanced up, he noticed the horns poking above Necra's head—the great yellow eye, positioned between the bars.

"Stanton!" he screamed. "Take the shot!"

Stanton's hands shook as he removed another syringe from his pocket and popped the cap. He supported his body against the gate and jammed the needle in the carnivore's eye.

Necra's screams rang louder as the *Carnotaurus* recoiled. A bony crunch echoed. Necra wrenched free from the animal's toothy snout. Caleb backed away. 44 cocked her head in curiosity as the woman stumbled and buried the gruesome stump of her wrist inside the fabric of her black tank top.

"Treachery!" Necra screamed. "Treachery! Vet bay! Treachery!"

Stanton was looking more coordinated as he pulled the huge metal pin from the *Carnotaurus* gate. Already Caleb heard the footfalls of approaching raiders. He helped Stanton pull the gate open. "44!" he shouted. "Over here!"

"Necra!" an approaching raider shouted. "What in bloody hell?"

"Look out!" another raider yelled.

Stanton and Caleb pulled the gate open wide. 44 swept behind them as the bull-head roared and emerged. Her eyes grew wide and bloodshot; the pupils swiftly dilated. Drool spilled between her teeth.

"Rogue bull!" the raiders shouted.

The *Carnotaurus* rampaged forward. She kicked Necra against a Triassica crate and chomped right, snagging one raider by the arm. She swung the screaming man like a pendulum and knocked the rest of the group on their backs.

Before the others could ready their shock prods, the *Carnotaurus* was already charging over them. More raiders retreated down the cavern, toward the hub. Screams and shouts and popping shock prods echoed amid the roar of the rampaging bull.

Once the large predator's armored tail disappeared down the tunnel, Stanton pushed the gate forward.

"You okay?" Caleb asked.

Stanton regarded Necra, face down in a pool of blood. He nodded. "I was only stunned. I'm good. You still have that claw?"

Caleb patted his side. "Maybe you should take this." He handed Stanton the shock prod.

"Thanks." Stanton nodded at the bodies strewn across the cavern. "Follow the carnage, and let's get out of here."

26

Stanton halted Caleb and 44 as they approached the hub. The scene was somehow a worse nightmare than anything they'd seen yet. The raging *Carnotaurus* charged like a locomotive. She pried open crates, swatted, snatched, and flung uncoordinated raiders.

What few shocks raiders could deliver sparked uselessly off her armored hide. The bull seemed immune to the pain. Stanton wondered how much higher his dosage had been than a bull unleashed on Columbia.

The bull made short work of the raiders brave enough to approach, snapping, stomping, and chewing them up.

Stanton almost felt sorry.

Almost.

He recalled how Ajax had felled the rogue bull in this very same cavern with surgical precision. *These raiders are not only not as good as Ajax, Necra, or even Caleb,* Stanton thought, mesmerized by the horror, *they're also drunk.*

Caleb eyed the metal ramp that led to the freight elevator.

"Wait," Stanton whispered. "Be patient. We'll never make it through all that unscathed."

They lurked and watched as more raiders were torn apart by the rampaging bull. Caleb slowly, carefully slipped his wrist claw over his right hand. His left hand affectionately scratched 44's neck feathers, keeping her calm.

At last, a group of four huge men surrounded the *Carnotaurus*. They cornered her with strategic shocks, to her arms, her snout, the tip of her tail. The *Carnotaurus* swirled like an armored tornado, snapping at them, only to suffer new shocks from the side and behind.

These men—perhaps sobered by adrenaline—knew just where to strike with maximum voltage.

While the four raiders circled the beast, Stanton scanned the hub, and surveyed the number of downed and dead raiders. It was nowhere near the amount that *should* have come charging out of the mess hall.

Relief coursed through him. The plan was working.

Finally, the *Carnotaurus* managed to chomp the head of one of the four strong men who had made their last stand. In that moment, the other three charged her snout and shocked her eyes.

Stanton looked away, suddenly sorry for the animal he had set loose, "like a bomb," as Caleb had explained it. When he glanced back, the three raiders standing were shoving their knives deep into the *Carnotaurus*'s eyes. The animal groaned and fell onto another crate of Columbia's ore that spilled and clanked into a sloppy pile.

The *Carnotaurus* moaned. Two of the surviving raiders panted and collapsed, hands on knees. The other one turned and spotted Stanton, Caleb, and 44. He pointed his bloody knife at Stanton and shouted. Then he stormed toward them.

Behind him, his two companions vomited uncontrollably.

Stanton readied his shock prod as the hulking raider approached, but before he was even halfway, the raider's eyes tilted back. His weapon quivered in his hand. He clutched his belly, doubled over, and puked black bile.

"Run!" Stanton commanded.

He and Caleb raced through the hub, around dead and dying raiders. Those who weren't mauled by the *Carnotaurus* lay pale and shivering. Anguished screams echoed from the mess hall.

They leapt over the tail of the fallen *Carnotaurus*. Her eyes were wet black pits. Her tiny forearms still twitched, batting chunks of ore to the ground.

They stomped up the metal ramp that led to the freight elevator. 44 crouched and crawled up the grooved surface.

"When we get to the top," Caleb said. "You get the jeep. I'll meet you."

"No splitting up," Stanton shouted.

"Trust me!"

A muscular shadow waited by the freight elevator. "Trust me?" the stony voice asked.

On either side of the Alpha stood two snarling, full-grown slashers.

"Trust, Caleb?" the Alpha snarled. "Trust is a cruel, sad joke."

27

The Alpha's human lips scowled in contrast to his inked *Carnotaurus* grin. The twin *Deinonychuses* were as tall as the Alpha, reminding Stanton just how small 44 was.

"Trust!" the Alpha spat the word out. "And faith and goodwill and nonsense! You call us murderers? *You* did this, Stanton! You killed my pack!"

"Necra's virus killed your pack," Stanton said calmly. "Caleb put it in the mead. And I never would have wanted him to do it, except…" Stanton shook his head. "This is what you would have done to our people. The cost of survival is steep, isn't it?"

The Alpha gave a slow, angry sigh. He attached his wrist claw. "I am going to gut you. And 28 and 29—perhaps the only creatures under this horn who will ever be worthy of my trust—they are going to tear your son's entrails from his stomach and devour him."

The two *Deinonychuses* gave sharp, angry barks.

"I'm not his son," Caleb hissed. "You killed my real parents. All of you."

The Alpha laughed and shook his head. "I knew it!" He sighed. "I was so sure until… you, Stanton, could negotiate with the devil, couldn't you?"

Stanton raised an eyebrow. "Isn't that what I've been doing?"

The Alpha thrust his claw, the two *Deinonychuses* leapt forward. One made a beeline for Stanton. The other darted toward Caleb and 44.

The Alpha followed the animal to his right. Stanton shielded his face with one arm and jabbed forward with his sawed dagger. A flurry of wiry, muscular claws, teeth, and red feathers writhed before him.

The *Deinonychus* attempted to push Stanton to the ground. His sickle-shaped toe claws scrounged for his groin. Stanton backed against the wall and slashed at the predator's neck. The slasher snorted and reared back; a clean red line streaked from the animal's throat to scaly shoulder. The wound was hardly deep, but it made the slasher study Stanton with newfound apprehension.

Over the animal's shoulders, he spotted 44 and Caleb, wrangling the other *Deinonychus*. Caleb expertly wriggled underneath his attacker and shoved his hunting knife deep into the animal's throat.

The Alpha's eyes widened with surprise as Caleb pushed the screeching, bleeding dinosaur into him.

Stanton used his free moment to charge his shock prod. He waited until the *Deinonychus* lurched forward again and jammed the tip into the gaping pink flesh of her open jaws. The predator's skull strobed electric blue. She toppled and twitched against the metal grating.

Caleb and the Alpha stood arm's length apart. The carcass of the other *Deinonychus* bled out behind the Alpha. He stabbed forward. Caleb rolled to safety.

44 leapt onto the Alpha's shoulders and gnawed the side of his face. The Alpha roared, grabbed the thick end of the small dinosaur's tail and hurled her onto the freight elevator.

The Alpha's back had been turned on Caleb for only a moment. Stanton's heart skipped a beat as Caleb screamed with fury and slashed forward.

The tips of the boy's claw scratched deep, leaving three red shreds across the bony vertebrae tattooed along his spine.

But the Alpha turned and backed away defensively. Caleb had failed to impale him.

The muscular man smacked Caleb hard in the jaw with his clawless knuckles. Caleb stumbled. A line of blood dribbled onto his boots. The Alpha grabbed the boy by the chin and hurled him against the wall.

Up the stairs! Stanton thought. *Make him follow you; don't give him time to finish Caleb.* Stanton's boots clanked up the steps.

"Oh yes!" The Alpha's laughter echoed. "Now you show your coward's belly, Stanton. Now that I know he's not your boy! Now you'll leave him!"

Stanton's lungs strained. He climbed higher and faster, uncoiling the rope from his belt as he rolled onto the first landing.

At the bottom of the steps, 44 screeched. Stanton tried to block out her pained yelps as the Alpha undoubtedly wrangled and tossed her aside like a ragdoll for a second time.

Instead, he worked faster than he ever had in his life, knotting, looping, securing, and laying out his trap. When he finished, he stood tall enough for the Alpha to see. He pretended to fumble at the keypad that unlocked the vehicle keys.

The Alpha stomped up the steps. "Who gave you the combos?" he asked. "Ajax, I assume. Still had that last little bit of breath in him, did he?"

Stanton watched out of the corner of his eye. The Alpha rose up the final step and strode forward, claw raised, ready to strike.

As soon as the Alpha stepped in his direction, Stanton yanked, hard as he could, and fell back against the wall.

The snare loop tightened around the Alpha's ankle and threw him off balance. Caleb came clanking up the steps.

Stanton pulled hard to his left, and the Alpha teetered over the railing.

Caleb charged with his shoulder.

For a moment, Stanton was certain that the Alpha would flip over the edge, but his biceps bulged as he managed to grip the bar with both hands. Astonishingly, he started to pull himself back over, grimacing with might.

Then 44 somersaulted from ground level and chomped the Alpha's neck. She dug her claws into his shoulders and weighed him back.

The Alpha screamed as he plummeted downward and snagged midair. A horrible snap echoed as the rope of the snare grew taut. The Alpha screamed and spun and dangled, his leg dislodged but attached by sinew and muscle.

44 landed nimbly on all fours on the surface of the elevator below.

The Alpha's agonized cries echoed off the walls. "You... you people..." he groaned. "*You* are the savages. *You* are! Come back down here! Finish what you started!"

Stanton unlocked the cabinet. Caleb reached for a set of keys labeled with the number 3.

"You little devil!" the Alpha said. "Come down and finish me!"

"You're already finished," Stanton said. "That claw Caleb scraped you with? The tips soaked all night in Necra's poison."

The Alpha fell silent. Horror and shame flooded his eyes.

"You're not the Alpha anymore," Stanton said. "You're nobody."

44 raced up the steps to join them. Caleb unstrapped the infected claw from his wrist and dropped it over the railing. It clanked on the metal below.

They climbed to the next landing as the Alpha's screams and roars echoed. Stanton pulled the lever and the panic gate grinded open, revealing a starry night sky.

Nearby, two raiders, sentries who had traded shifts toward the end of dinner, lay pale and shivering in the dirt, already succumbing to the virus. The Alpha's screams died away as Stanton, Caleb, and 44 rushed toward the vehicle lot.

Stanton glanced nervously at the lookout tower atop the east horn, but nothing up there stirred. *We got all of them,* he thought. *If there is a god, I hope he forgives me, but I have to believe it was the only way.*

"Start the car!" Caleb shouted. "Meet me at the tunnel!"

"Caleb, no!"

"I'll be fast." Caleb rushed toward the tunnel that cut through the boulder field. 44 scampered after him.

Stanton shook his head. No sense arguing with the boy now. He found the jeep with a black "3" spray-painted on its side and unhitched the flatbed trailer, which would only slow them down. He leapt inside and inserted the key.

The battery hummed to life. The dash lit up.

The headlights flared, and Stanton kicked up dust as he peeled away from the lot and backed toward the shadowy tunnel under the boulders.

His heart pounded. "Come on, Caleb, come on."

A series of roars split the night. Caleb and 44 came racing through the tunnel. Two looming *Carnotauruses* were hot on their heels. "Go!" Caleb screamed. "Go! Go! Go!" He leapt onto the back of the jeep, and 44 leapt clear over him into the passenger seat.

Stanton shifted gears and accelerated.

Two bull-heads came snapping out of the tunnel. In the red glow of the taillights, Stanton spotted *Deinonychuses* pouring out from behind the large predators, sniffing and searching.

The bulls seemed to lose interest as they raced down the winding path away from the horns. The freed dinosaurs started searching among the vehicles, investigating the open gates to the raiders' stronghold.

Caleb climbed into the passenger seat and threw his arms around 44. He shouted with joy.

"I wish you hadn't done that," Stanton said. Then he laughed. "But… I'm sort of glad you did."

"Wouldn't be right," Caleb said. "To leave all those bulls and slashers locked up with nobody to feed them."

"They'll go back to what's natural now, I guess," Stanton said.

Caleb gave a long, satisfied sigh. He leaned back in his seat. 44 rested her snout in his lap. "What about you?" Caleb scratched his pet's feathers. "What are you going back to?"

"Good question," Stanton said. "First stop, Columbia. We'll tell them everything that happened. Let them know that the raiders' eastern camp has been neutralized. We can help them organize an armed expedition to come back here, reclaim what they stole, and make sure that virus doesn't end up in the wrong hands."

"Then what?" Moonlight glowed over Caleb's tattooed eye. His smile broadened. He looked every bit as tough as the kid who had saved him in the storage garage, but a heck of a lot happier.

"Then," Stanton said. "I am going back to Triassica to file a report. I'll let them know that with the raiders crippled, they no longer have any reason to withdraw support from Columbia. And then… I'm going to resign."

"You're good at what you do, though," Caleb said. "Negotiating. Figuring people out."

"There may be better ways to use that gift," Stanton said. "I am entitled to a payout of resources if I give up my place in the compound. I figure… maybe I can bounce around the south a little. Be my own boss. It won't be easy, though."

"Nothing's easy in New Pangea," Caleb said.

"You got that right, kid." Stanton said. "Survival is a full-time gig. You and 44 interested in a job?"

Caleb smiled. 44 chittered at the sound of her name. "We work together pretty good." He held out his hand, and Stanton shook it.

"Your father would be proud of you, Caleb."

"So would yours."

28

Necra was always careful in her every action, but she could not recall the last time she had to move with such agonizing slowness. She held her wound high, and with fleeting ounces of strength, gripped the fabric of her shirt to minimize blood loss.

Many times, as she crawled through the hub, over the dead and dying members of her pack, she felt she would pass away in exhaustion. But slowly, surely, she made it into the mess hall and clawed her way to the kitchen.

She propped herself against the stove, turned the flame on all the way, and seared the flesh of her severed wrist.

The pain was unbearable. Once again, she was certain she would black out and slip away forever.

But Necra did not die.

I am a survivor, she reminded herself, over and over. *I am a survivor.*

She pined for water, but she did not trust the food or drink that surrounded her as she crawled back out of the mess hall. *Stanton.* The name writhed through her mind like a poison serpent. *Stanton infected them all.*

She recognized the symptoms of bull fever around her. She could not waste time now worrying about exactly how he had done it.

She only knew to drink or eat nothing under the horn.

She crawled.

And she crawled.

Her head rocked with vertigo when she at last made it past the vet bay to the elevator shaft. For a minute, she blanked out. But miraculously, she came to when the elevator jolted at the top of the west horn.

Necra crawled onto the surface of the horn. Gray clouds rolled over the badlands and blended with the purple sky of pre-dawn.

She screeched as loud as she could, her voice weary and weak. She was sure that nothing would hear.

But her *Pteranodon* landed and chittered with concern. Necra wrapped her arms around the flyer's leathery neck and pulled herself to her knees. With one hand she struggled to unfasten the burlap strap and remove a small blank piece of paper. She found a piece of charcoal on the ground, broken, but still sharp, and scrawled as legibly as she could.

Stanton. Kill him. Find me. Treachery. Columbia. Triassica. I am…

She shuddered, then finished the note:

I am Alpha now.

Then she felt she could write no more. She tucked the message inside the pouch and secured it. "Yah!" She slapped the ground and thrust the finger of her remaining hand skyward.

The *Pteranodon* launched into the air and sailed toward the clouds.

Necra sprawled onto her back. She rested the charred, burning stump of her wrist in the palm of the hand that remained. Her mouth was dry as the badlands that surrounded her.

If I die here, she thought. *The pterosaurs will smell my rotting flesh. They will come to pick at me.* Tears streamed down her cheeks. *I will die like my father.*

She shuddered at that thought. Her tongue scraped the roof of her mouth.

Thunder rumbled.

And then it rained.

Clean, nourishing rain.

AUTHOR'S NOTE

On the history of New Pangea...

Long ago, human settlers arrived in New Pangea, a place where the magnificent animals of the Mesozoic era thrive. Exactly why these humans fled their ancestral home across unfathomable boundaries remains a mystery. Overpopulation? Lack of resources? Sheer adventure? Perhaps all the above.

Those colonists came armed with knowledge of ancient life, a treasure trove of seeds, and only the technology that mattered most for survival. Time, tribalism, and the ravages of nature would fracture them across generations. Ancestral books became a precious commodity after the great diaspora.

The footprint of an invasive humanity altered a tapestry of Triassic, Jurassic, and Cretaceous ecosystems. And for better or worse, native dinosaurs would be forever adapting to the burgeoning infrastructure of their human neighbors.

To me, as an author, New Pangea is many things. A backdrop for adventure. An imagined sanctuary for spectacular animals. But also, a very real place, with a life as untamable as its inhabitants. I'm glad to have discovered a shared world to explore whenever a dinosaur wanders into the spotlight of my creativity, and I certainly owe my inspiration to people like J.R.R. Tolkien, Michael Crichton, Arthur Conan Doyle, and many more. As Crichton's Ian Malcolm would surely point out, I'm standing on the shoulders of geniuses, but what else can we do as a species? In that regard, New Pangea has become a fascinating thought experiment to me as well. How would we survive in a prehistoric environment? What would we need? How much would we get in our own way, and who should be more afraid, the humans or the dinosaurs?

For the people born on New Pangea, it's home. It's the only life they know, and most of them are too busy trying to survive deadly carnivores to uncover the secrets of their past.

I understand that readers may wish to know a little more.

There is more. I suspect a lot more. But for now, I welcome you to view these breathtaking and terrifying animals through the eyes of my characters. Hopefully, we'll continue learning about New Pangea together, one exciting tale at a time!

Kevin M. Folliard
Chicagoland, 2022

ABOUT THE AUTHOR

Kevin M. Folliard is a Chicagoland writer whose fiction has been collected by The Horror Tree, Flame Tree Publishing, The Dread Machine, and more. His recent publications include his novella "Tower of Raven" from Demain Publishing, his 2020 horror anthology *The Misery King's Closet*, and his YA fantasy adventure novel *Grayson North: Frost-Keeper of the Windy City*, the latter from Dark Owl Publishing. Kevin currently resides in the western suburbs of Chicago, Illinois, where he enjoys his day job in academia and membership in the La Grange and Brookfield Writers Groups. When not writing or working, he's usually reading Stephen King, playing Super Mario Maker, or traveling the U.S.A.

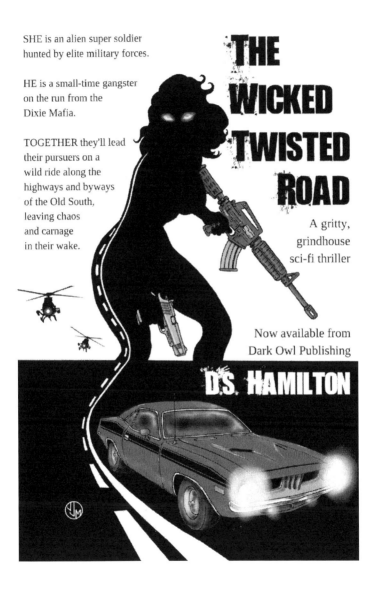

SHE is an alien super soldier
hunted by elite military forces.

HE is a small-time gangster
on the run from the
Dixie Mafia.

TOGETHER they'll lead
their pursuers on a
wild ride along the
highways and byways
of the Old South,
leaving chaos
and carnage
in their wake.

THE
WICKED
TWISTED
ROAD

A gritty,
grindhouse
sci-fi thriller

Now available from
Dark Owl Publishing

D.S. HAMILTON

THE LAST STAR WARDEN

"A rare and refreshing level of pure pulpy fun."

~ Gregory L. Norris. Author of the Gerry Anderson's Into Infinity novels

TALES OF ADVENTURE AND MYSTERY VOLUME I

THE PHANTOM WORLD NOVELLA

THE UN QUAN SAGA VOLUME II

NOW AVAILABLE!
PAPERBACK AND KINDLE

NOW SERIALIZED
ON KINDLE VELLA
FIRST 3 EPISODES ARE FREE!

NOW AVAILABLE!
PAPERBACK AND KINDLE

Written and Illustrated by

JASON J. MCCUISTON

Author of Project Notebook

For more details and to order, visit Dark Owl Publishing

www.darkowlpublishing.com

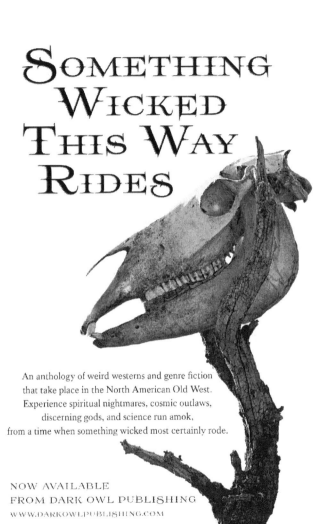

We all know how the stories go:

An unlikely hero will gather a member of every race and every nation
to discover the Fallen Lord's dark secret and cause his defeat.
But Adal is the most unlikely of heroes,
and the stories must be satisfied with the company he leads.

Will the Fallen Lord turn the tales
of the Storied Lands against them?

THE KEEPER OF TALES

STORIES ARE ALIVE.
THEY WILL BE TOLD.

an epic fantasy adventure by

JONATHON MAST

Now Available
in paperback and on Kindle
Dark Owl Publishing, LLC
www.darkowlpublishing.com
Where quality fiction comes to nest.

Made in the USA
Columbia, SC
17 September 2022

67117947R00143